eradication

ALSO BY JONATHAN MILES

Dear American Airlines

Want Not

Anatomy of a Miracle: The True* Story of a Paralyzed Veteran, a Mississippi Convenience Store, a Vatican Investigation, and the Spectacular Perils of Grace

eradication

JONATHAN MILES

riverrun

First published in the United States in 2026 by Penguin Random House LLC
First published in Great Britain in 2026 by riverrun

an imprint of Quercus
Part of John Murray Group

1

Copyright © 2026 Jonathan Miles

The moral right of Jonathan Miles to be
identified as the author of this work has been
asserted in accordance with the Copyright,
Designs and Patents Act 1988.

All rights reserved. No part of this publication
may be reproduced or transmitted in any form
or by any means, electronic or mechanical,
including photocopy, recording, or any
information storage and retrieval system,
without permission in writing from the publisher.

This book is a work of fiction. Names, characters,
businesses, organizations, places and events are
either the product of the author's imagination
or used fictitiously. Any resemblance to
actual persons, living or dead, events or
locales is entirely coincidental.

A CIP catalogue record for this book is available
from the British Library

HB ISBN 978 1 52944 903 7
EBOOK ISBN 978 1 52944 905 1

Offset in 13.10/18.08pt Adobe Caslon Pro by Six Red Marbles UK, Thetford, Norfolk

Printed and bound in Great Britain by Clays Ltd, Elcograf S.p.A.

Papers used by Quercus are from well-managed forests and other responsible sources.

Quercus
Carmelite House
50 Victoria Embankment
London EC4Y 0DZ

John Murray Group
Part of Hodder & Stoughton Limited
An Hachette UK company

The authorised representative in the EEA is Hachette Ireland,
8 Castlecourt Centre, Dublin 15, D15 XTP3, Ireland (email: info@hbgi.ie)

For my goatherders

TOM RANKIN

&

MATTHEW TEAGUE

Captain Hannah had it right: heaven is *pals.*

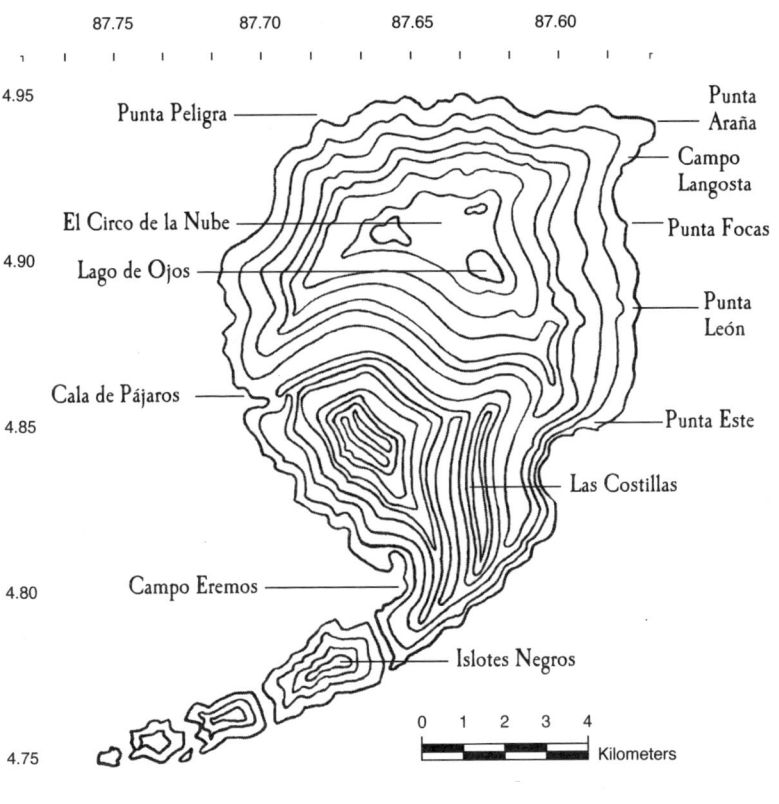

FIGURE 2. Santa Flora Island, with place names used in this flora. Based on USDMA Chart 22997, 12th edition, 1982.

eradication

The first sailor was beefy and tall and already sweating before the sun was risen. The second sailor was missing.

He'll be along, the first sailor told Adi. With a flashlight jammed between his teeth he was filling out clipboarded forms and humming what sounded like a melody braked to quarter-speed, groany and dirgelike and, for Adi, unsettling in the predawn dark. The boat, a thirty-foot center console with two giant outboard motors, kept thunking the dock where Adi stood as the sailor went rummaging about the deck, opening and closing storage hatches to dash items from his checklist. *He'll be along,* he repeated, though to whom it was unclear.

After a while the sailor clapped his hands together and motioned to Adi's gear on the dock, which Adi handed down: two fat duffels, a backpack, four cellophane-sealed boxes, a pair of heavy plastic crates, a satellite phone pack, and a long thin black case secured with padlocks. There was no mistaking the latter as anything but a rifle case, and the sailor's hum shifted to a pitchy song of vigilance as it got passed over the water. He parked it with the rest of the gear at the boat's stern and then stood for several awkward moments shining his flashlight up at Adi.

You're not a scientist.

No. Adi squinted, his fingers splayed against the flashlight beam. *I'm not.*

At this the sailor lowered his light, frowning. But soon he was nodding at Adi and grinning. *Then you're an assassin,* he said, pantomiming a rifle shot. Adi could see the sailor's broad teeth shining in the dark. *A sharpshooter.*

Adi shrugged.

A killer, the sailor went on, but this time so acidly that Adi found himself unable to muster any response, not even another shrug.

Just then a pair of headlights entered the harbor. Adi and the sailor watched a taxi thread its way to the dock gate, where a man dragged himself from the back seat and stood swaying, counting out bills for the driver. From the deck the first sailor snorted. *I told you he'd be along,* he said, but again it was unclear to whom.

The second sailor came swerving down the dock toward the boat. The first sailor whistled low and confirmed what Adi was thinking. *He's shitfaced.*

You're shitfaced! he shouted.

The second sailor brushed by Adi and wobbled onto the deck. This was the mate, Adi deduced, making the first sailor the captain. Short and bald and snake-hip skinny, the mate was the physical opposite of the captain, as in silent-movie comedy duos. He had to steady himself against the pilothouse to tuck his shirt into his pants. Only half made it in.

You're straight from Angel's, aren't you? the captain said.

The mate blew the air from his cheeks and then, sour-faced, placed a palm on his chest, as though he'd tried and failed to expel something.

The captain growled, *You haven't even been home.*

The mate ignored him and set himself to work. He hoisted the national flag along with another flag bearing the naval insignia. He unfolded a seat near the stern and with sharp impatient gestures motioned for Adi to board. He freed the dock lines and coiled the ropes and hauled in the fenders while inside the small open pilothouse the captain fired the engines and hummed his drowsy song.

How long will it take us? Adi asked him.

Santa Flora? Six hours. More humming. *Maybe longer. Some chop in the water today.*

Over the rooftops of the town was rising a thin stripe of dawn. The captain piloted the boat out of the harbor into the slate-colored sea.

Yes, Santa Flora! the captain shouted to the mate, who was leaning over the port-side gunwale, licking his lips. *A nice long cruise. We should have music and beer, like at Angel's.*

We should, said the mate, though his curdled expression disagreed.

Half an hour or more passed before anyone spoke again. The captain sipped coffee and hummed and, when the radio squawked, sometimes tilted his thick head toward it. Adi found himself watching the mate, who, pressing his palms to the gunwale, kept dipping his head toward the water. From his lips swung a long rope of drool flickering neon green in the navigation lights' glow. Adi had presumed that sailors would be immune to seasickness, but then Adi had not been around sailors before. For that matter he'd never been on a boat before, not counting the paddleboats at the capital zoo and a sunset river cruise he'd once taken with his wife. So he didn't know.

When the captain spoke again, it was as though

the previous conversation, about music and beer, had not ended—that it'd merely been paused without anyone's thoughts drifting in the interim. *And some girls too,* he said. *Wouldn't that be nice?*

It would, groaned the mate.

Cha cha, said the captain, swishing his backside. *Cha cha cha.*

Ahead Adi saw only bluish-gray water and grayish-blue sky, the water whitecapped, the sky starflecked. Behind the boat, though, was brewing a sunrise unlike any he could remember seeing: gorgeous and streaky like some big-budget advertisement for divinity, the sky slashed with ribbons of orange and rose and peach and gold and the boat's deck blushing pink in its reflection. In other company Adi might've pointed to it, voiced his awe. But the sailors had clearly seen it, and were as clearly unimpressed.

Over the rim of his coffee cup the captain was grinning at the mate, whose head now drooped overboard. *Who were you with at Angel's, huh?*

Weakly, the mate waved him off.

I'll bet Chita, the captain said. *It was Chita, wasn't it?*

The mate's body heaved.

It's always Chita with you.

Into the sea went a gush of his insides.

The captain laughed while the mate sputtered and

gagged. *Poor Chita,* he said. He lit a thin cigar and shook out the match. *I am going to tell her you retch at just the mention of her name. I'm going to ask her if she thinks this means love.*

Again the mate waved him off, before another spout of vomit left him.

We should ask Mister Killer here, the captain said, aiming his cigar at Adi. *Should love make you retch?*

The word *killer* piqued the mate. With watery eyes and a glazed chin he lifted his head to assess Adi, who knew he didn't square with anyone's image of a killer. He looked instead like what he had been until eleven months ago: a schoolteacher, an amateur jazz clarinetist, a husband, a father. The mate sat blinking at him.

I guess it depends on the love, Adi finally answered.

Yes! the captain shouted, as the mate went back to dangling his head overboard. *It depends on the love.* He nibbled his cigar and mulled this awhile, having mistaken Adi's circumspection for profundity. Then with mock courtroom gravity he addressed the mate: *Will you define for Mister Killer the nature of your love for Chita?*

As if on cue, the mate retched again.

What could *he love about her?* The captain frowned, mimicking thought. *Maybe it's her hair. Chita has very nice hair.* He wiggled his fingers around his head and grinned at the mate, who did not grin back. *Silky silky.*

He hummed awhile.

Or maybe, let's see—maybe it's that magnificent cyst on her shoulder? He turned to Adi, cupping a hand as if holding an invisible grapefruit. *It's enormous. You half expect it to talk, like a pirate's parrot.*

The mate wiped his chin with his forearm, muttering.

No, said the captain, and shook his head and sighed. *I suspect the true nature of his love for Chita is that Chita charges less than the other girls at Angel's.*

Adi flushed and turned away, pretending to study something on the horizon.

It is a great romance, the captain went on. *Like Romeo and Juliet, I think. But different. Isn't that right, Bruno?*

The mate, drooling into the sea, hoisted a middle finger.

At this the captain laughed, but gently now, almost affectionately, as though some sort of abiding private ritual had been concluded, a routine punishment meted. He suckled his thin cigar and hummed some more before turning back to Adi.

And what about you? Is there a Mrs. Killer?

Adi lowered his eyes.

Ah, well. The captain shrugged. *This is good. Otherwise you'd be sad to be leaving her today. You'd be annoying us with all your boohooing.*

The risen sun was burning off the last of the fleecy clouds and all the world was blue and getting bluer. Hours passed. The captain's forecast for choppy seas had proven accurate, and the boat's hull kept smacking the water instead of gliding through it. To keep from getting bounced overboard Adi stood gripping the pilothouse roof and pinning his foot soles to the deck, bending at the knees with each spumy slap, his jaw clenched to keep his teeth from knocking.

Then he saw the captain motioning, corkscrewing a finger toward the stern.

Three porpoises were chasing the boat, diving in and out of the frothy wake. They were sleek and silver and to Adi seemed magical as mermaids. Soon a fourth porpoise appeared, larger and higher-flying than the others, and for a jittery moment, as it came swiveling through the spindrift, Adi feared it might leap onto the deck. When it didn't Adi whistled and wagged his head as though astonished by an athletic feat, by a gymnast sticking some implausible landing.

But as the porpoises kept tailing the boat a hazier anxiety began unsettling him. Why were the porpoises doing this? Their expressions—glimpsed briefly through the spray—were impenetrable to him. Were they stalking the boat like wolves, to attack it? Or like carrier pigeons, to warn of something? Or were they mobbing it, like gulls, to drive it away?

He looked to the captain, who must've sensed his bewilderment. *They're playing. Like street dogs chasing cars.*

Adi nodded and resumed watching until the captain barked to the mate: *Hide his gun, Bruno! Mister Killer wants to shoot them!*

Adi spun toward the captain, whose rubbery grin was overspreading his face and whose eyebrows were jumping and dancing with a caustic strain of delight.

That's not true, Adi protested. *Don't say that.*

With his thumb and forefinger the captain mimed a pistol shot toward the stern. *Ka-blam.* Then, with a crooked smile, he fanned his hands in a cavalier shrug.

Killers kill, he said.

The wounded glare Adi leveled at him seemed to take the captain by surprise. With popped eyes and an emphatic chop he motioned to himself and the helm. *Like sailors sail!*

He squirmed and sputtered, until:

And like mates, hooking a thumb toward Bruno, . . . *mate.*

The blast of laughter that followed was as though

two bombs detonated on the boat, one big, the other small. The captain yowled and stomped and with tears in his eyes staggered to Bruno and repeated what he'd said, *like mates mate,* the captain's body jellied with glee and the hungover mate convulsing with high-pitched wheezes, the two of them punching and pawing each other until they collapsed into a lopsided embrace—a junction of dumb rapture that struck Adi as even more alien than whatever the dolphins were up to behind the boat. He glanced back to check on them. It seemed possible the dolphins were laughing too.

Only the sight of Santa Flora on the horizon quelled the hysterics. As soon as Adi alerted them to the distant gray bulge the sailors wiped their eyes and smoothed their shirts and comported themselves like naval officers again. As the island came into sharper view, less a gray bulge now than a beige spearhead, an abrupt and orderly calm seized the boat. Even for himself, Adi couldn't say whether this calm stemmed from wonder or fear or reverence or dread or merely from the visual cue of the day's mission, like a factory whistle summoning lunching workers back to their stations. The captain snapped orders and the mate executed them. Adi turned to see what the porpoises were doing but the porpoises were gone.

On the maps Adi had studied, Santa Flora resembled a comma on an otherwise blank page, but from the boat, as they made their westerly approach, he couldn't distinguish the comma's head from its tail; to his eye it was all just a uniformly scarpy chunk of land heaved from the sea that, lacking soft slopes or beaches or verdure or really any colors besides khaki and ash and a sparse dingy olive, gave the impression of not wanting to be bothered, of a primordial indifference. From every approach its back seemed turned.

Once we get around the south cape we'll be landing you at Eremos Cove, the captain told him. *There's just two landing sites on the island. The other is Campo Langosta on the north end, but only at high tide, and Punta Araña can be dicey to get around. You might see fishing boats if you're up there. They're illegal. Shark finners from up north. Nasty bastards.*

They followed the cliff-indented shoreline south until the comma's tail petered into a curl of volcanic stacks, dozens and dozens of clustered rock formations like half-submerged ruins of ancient statuary. Then the captain hooked the boat back northward, humming his dreary song while Adi and the mate stood flanking him. Beneath the midday sun the island appeared blanched and shadowless, like an unfinished painting.

You'll see where we dropped you your water last week, the captain told Adi. *Half a pallet of it! Enough for you to make a bubble bath every night.* He cocked a bushy eyebrow. *Your foundation must have deep pockets.*

The captain slid the boat between a pair of contorted rock spires and into the cove called Eremos. The water here was instantly different—turquoise and stilly—as was the coastline, with a narrow orange beach and clumps of what looked like palm trees bunched in the shallows and scattered amid another species of spindly misshapen trees. Adi saw where the sailors had left the half pallet of bottled water on their earlier trip, stacked right beside a primitive hut that he'd been told about, and this abrupt combination of shade, shelter, and gently lapping water relaxed something inside him. The island remained far from welcoming but at least here it wasn't scowling.

The captain burbled the boat as close to the beach as he could get while the mate dropped the bow anchor. Then the mate leapt into the waist-high water and, carrying the stern anchor, towed the boat in closer to moor it in the sand. He waded back and clapped his hands twice. The captain passed the mate one of Adi's duffels, which he hauled to the beach, and in this way, item by item, the sailors began moving Adi onto the island.

The rifle case and Adi himself were the last of these items to go.

Your taxi here will be back for you in five weeks, the captain told him. *Maybe we'll bring beer for you! You'd like that, yes? But then Bruno might drink it all.*

Adi and the mate sploshed toward the beach, side by side but without speaking, the rifle case hoisted above the mate's head, his jaw clamped shut and his eyes still pained-looking.

Enjoy yourself, Mister Killer, the captain called from the stern. *You're going to put some damn holes in the island, aren't you? Ha! You might sink it!*

Once on land the mate leaned the rifle case against Adi's pile of gear and seemed to study it for a while. Then he screwed his red eyes at Adi, at the cragged slopes rising behind the beach, then at Adi again, and asked, *You really get to kill them all?*

For the second time that day Adi found himself unable to muster a response. Only later, in the disorienting silence of an otherwise unpeopled island, did it occur to Adi that the mate might've said *got*, not *get*.

The job listing hadn't mentioned killing. What it had mentioned, rather, was saving the world. And Adi liked the sound of that. What'd attracted him even more was five weeks of solo work in a remote, uninhabited location. Just imagining it felt restorative, medicinal, antidotal. He'd called the number and set up an interview.

The foundation's offices were on a high floor in a glassy rhomboid building in the capital. The foundation funded programs in medicine, education, civil society, and conservation, Adi's interviewer told him, with offices all over the world. *São Paulo, Berlin, Lagos, Washington, Sydney.* She had butterscotch skin and oversized glasses and spoke with a peculiarly lilting accent that sounded knitted together from the languages of at least three continents. *Dubai, London, Stockholm, Johannesburg, Singapore.* She might've been from any one of those cities or from all of them.

She led him to a chrome desk, where she shuffled some papers until, with a soft, pleased grunt, she plucked the one she'd been seeking. *So,* she said, *right,* skimming. *You're here about the eradication op. The Santa Flora post.*

Adi hoped his expression wasn't as blank as it felt. *The . . . saving the world ad . . . the five-week—*

Right right, that's the one. A thin smile. *That's our labor engagement coordinator. Jasper loves using the come-save-the-world line. He's not wrong, though, is he? It does snatch the eyeballs.*

Adi squirmed. This side note of hers felt prematurely collegial and weirdly cynical. Who wouldn't want to save the world?

Though in this case, she went on, *it happens to be true in an unusually literal way. Not the whole world but for sure a worthy knob of it.* She flattened her palms on the desktop and leaning forward asked him, *How much do you know about Santa Flora?*

He bit his lip. Every year he'd made his fourth graders memorize the country's islands, so, not untruthfully, he answered: *A little bit.*

Then you know about the goats.

He raised an index finger, a lifelong reflex when bewildered. *The . . .*

The goats.

Oh, dropping the finger. *Sure,* he lied.

It's so much worse than what you might've read in the government reports. She shook her head, almost a shiver. *Frankly, at this point—the island's close to a bare rock. I mean, this was a landscape Melville wrote about. William Dampier. Dampier called it a chunk of Eden that must've floated off before the Fall. Two hundred years ago it was covered in cloud forest and home to absolutely immense seal and seabird colonies. So many birds that one explorer claimed you* heard *Santa Flora before you ever saw it. And now—it's just—it's barren.*

Again Adi's finger went up. His mother used to say the finger was his subconscious pointing to God for an explanation. *Because of . . .*

Because of the goats, right.

Because they . . . ?

Well, because they've eaten everything. Ravished every bloody stem of it.

Adi nodded, and as he processed what she was saying his finger descended. For a moment he thought he might see the outlines of the job becoming clear: the foundation was in need of someone to plant food crops for famished goats, likely something sturdier and more prolific and faster growing than the island's native plants. Or maybe the job would be to hand-feed them, the way he imagined farmers must do. Something had gone out of whack on Santa Flora and its goats needed rescuing. In the foundation's calculus, he guessed, saving goats equaled saving the world: a stretch, perhaps, but then apparently that's how Jasper won the job fairs.

Yet it didn't quite click. Why would a global foundation care about the fate of livestock on an uninhabited island? Back up went the finger. *The goats . . . they aren't native, are they?*

She almost spit. *God no, they aren't native.* Warping her face was the expression people tend to reserve for foul odors. *The Santa Flora Ground Dragon, that was native. Extinct now. The Blue-Crested Rail, also native, also bloody extinct. The Santa Flora Reed Warbler, extinct. The Santa Flora whiptail skink, extinct. Thirty-two endemic plant species: extinct. No, the goats aren't native. They're invasive. They're a fucking plague.*

Feeding goats, Adi deduced, would not be part of the job.

And of course we've got the whalers to thank for them, she said, and in response to his fuddled look she went on: *They'd drop off breeding pairs on their way to the hunting grounds, as a way to ensure themselves some fresh meat. You dumped some goats on an island, you sailed off to kill your whales, the goats did as goats do, and on your way back you stopped off to slaughter some for the trip home. Like a drive-through.*

Whaling, Adi echoed. The word evoked blacksmithing, telegraphing, wainwrighting: terms crusted with obsolescence. *That was a long time ago.*

Well, we can't get much past you, can we now? Her intent was a gentle jibe—a wink and crooked smile followed—but Adi stiffened his grip on the armrests and exhaled through his nose. His skin had never been thick but in the last few months it'd never been thinner. *But you're not wrong,* she said. *That's nineteenth-century history, it is. The problem is that history leaves a slime trail, like a snail. Whaling eventually ended, more or less. But the goats didn't. No one thought about them except a few sealers and fishermen stopping off at Santa Flora. The goats ate, they made more of each other, the new ones ate alongside the old. The airplane was invented. The goats looked up, chewing. The atomic bomb got dropped. The goats glanced over, chewing. Humans walked on the moon. The goats kept chewing. Birds stopped landing on Santa Flora because there were no more trees for them but without any other islands in range entire species fell from the sky and disappeared. Birdsong was no longer the predominant sound on Santa Flora. The grinding of teeth was.*

Now Adi understood, or thought he did. The goats didn't need saving. The island itself needed saving—from them. *How many goats are there?*

At one point there may have been forty thousand of them. But after most of the vegetation was denuded—sometime around the 1920s, I think—the population crashed. Our best estimate is that there are two to four thousand goats on Santa Flora. Just enough to keep the vegetation in a perpetual state of buzz cut.

Wow, said Adi, but wagging her head and pursing her lips she made clear to him that astonishment wasn't the proper response. *I mean, it's not anything new out there,* she said. *Of course it isn't. We've seen it a hundred times in the Pacific, right? Galápagos. Raoul. Guadalupe. Catastrophes all. Until now there's just never been the public and private capital to address Santa Flora.*

None of this was aligning, in Adi's head, with what the job listing had delineated: five weeks of solo work, it'd said. Two to four thousand goats and one person doing—what?

So how do you save it? he asked.

Save?

Santa Flora, he said, and gesturing vaguely toward her paperwork he added, *the world.*

Oh. Right. A crisp nod. *Well, the good news is that it's actually quite easy. You remove the goats.*

Remove them how?

By eradicating them.

Eradicating them how?

You shoot them. Her mouth a straight line. *All of them.*

Who does?

Well, you, she said. *If you turn out to be a fit for the operation.*

That's the job? His mouth a circle. *Shooting goats?*

No, she said. *That's not the job.* She drew a long steeling breath through her nose. *The job is saving one of the Pacific Ocean's most unique and vibrant ecosystems from very certain destruction. The job is removing a malignant growth that's been steadily erasing some of the most vulnerable and least studied flora and fauna on the bloody planet. The job is rescuing one of the most devastated seabird habitats in the Pacific. The job is preventing the assured extinction of at least eight more species of birds and five more species of reptiles and an entirely unknown number of plants. That's the job. That's what it is.*

She fell back into her chair with an aggravated windedness, as though explaining this point to him had been unnecessary labor, a gratuitous emotional sap. She was glaring not so much at Adi as through him, as though standing behind him was a sneering billy goat munching some endangered flower. At some point, however, she must've noticed Adi's mouth still flopped open.

It's not easy work but it's noble work. She angled

toward him, her tone gentler now. *Poisoning isn't an option, for the obvious downstream reasons. Mass sterilization isn't remotely possible, same as capture. But here's the thing. Hardly anything else we do here yields results this . . . tangible. We can buy a quarter million hectares of rainforest and arm five hundred monitors to protect it but ultimately that's just holding a line. It stops more losses, right, but nothing's gained. This is different. With this, you'll be able to take your children or grandchildren to Santa Flora and say, listen to those birds, look at those trees. I did this. Me. I brought this back from the dead.*

She let Adi sit with this for a while. Then she dipped her head forward, smiling, as though peeking at him from under a wide hat brim. *Is that something you might like?*

Was it? He stared downward, flicking at his pant leg. Resurrector of the dead. Savior of birdsong and reptile shade. A reverse Saint Patrick. Who wouldn't like that? Might as well ask: Would you like to be invisible, would you like rewinding time, would you like someone loving you and loving you forever? Not the whole world, she'd said, but for sure a worthy knob of it. His nod was hesitant but her smile widened anyway.

Lightly, in a make-talk way, she asked, *So do you have any children?*

A long pause. *I did.*

This pulled her up short. The way he'd said it, like he'd spoken shadows. She wobbled her head, lips slightly parted, weighing the air, deciding whether to probe. Instead she slid a notepad across the desk and, *click,* thumbed the end of a pen. *Now then,* she said, *right, getting on, you do have military or law enforcement experience?*

Adi shook his head foggily, still steeped in the previous two questions and the kindred question of whether he could actually do this, if he could shoot, could kill. He'd been asked to pick up a gun one previous time in his life, and refused. It hadn't ended well.

She said, *On the listing I think we said military or law enforcement preferred.*

I figured preferred *just meant,* blinking, opening his hands, *preferred.*

Fair enough. But you have firearms experience?

A bit, trying not to blanch.

Right then. Enough, you'd say?

Enough? He rubbed his hands against his pant legs. *Sure.*

Expeditionary experience? Comfortable outdoors?

She'd granted him a wide spectrum there. Adi's nod came easily.

More questions came and more answers followed.

Filling the job had evidently been proving difficult for them. The pay was negligible and the conditions extreme. It occurred to Adi that perhaps Jasper wasn't quite the employment savant that she'd suggested. The people who might relish such an assignment—he was thinking of his soon-to-be ex-wife's thuggish cousins, who enjoyed taking drunken potshots at rats—were unlikely to be lured by a cryptic save-the-world come-on, while those enticed by the calling, like Adi, might flinch at the job's duties and contradictions. After a while he got the feeling that the foundation's choice might be between him and nobody, between him and more extinctions. *Turn off the oven*, like his friend Matias used to say, watching a lopsided football game, *this one's cooked.*

She asked, *Do you have any mental conditions you feel you should disclose?*

Now it was Adi's turn to pull up short. Into his mind flashed another memory of Matias, glancing sideways, hands in his pockets, suggesting Adi see *some kind of doctor*, both of them knowing which kind he meant. His sister, Ana, her round face wrecked with pity, urging him to *talk to someone*. The headmaster at his school requesting Adi take a sabbatical, *under the circumstances*. Did all of that constitute a condition? Was grief a condition? Was heartbreak? Was an all-consuming desire to flee the red pain of the world, flee its people, your memories, your life—was that a condition and if so what was its name?

Just the same ones we all have, Adi mumbled, and the interviewer hiked her eyebrows and bobbed her head and laughed and scribbled something in her notepad and five minutes later told Adi he was hired.

A single glance upward made clear to Adi why he was here. The steep hillsides were trampled and grazed and stubbled with wizened-looking bushes that in their defoliated state resembled a crop of menorahs. This desert island looked, indeed, like a desert. Remnants of the great cloud forests supposedly still existed on the island, but from Eremos Cove, at least, they weren't visible. What was visible—almost everywhere, once you started looking—were goats.

Adi had never seen a goat before—never in the flesh, anyway. His entire life had been spent in the capital, where rivers flowed through concrete channels, flowers bloomed in window pots, and trees rose from squares cut from the sidewalk. At the zoo, as a child, he'd seen giraffes and lions and monkeys and crocodiles, but the zoo didn't exhibit livestock like sheep and goats, or if it did Adi and his family had never bothered seeing them. In his lifetime in the city he'd encountered a multitude of dogs—none of them his own, because of his mother's allergies—and a million pigeons and a few hundred rats and once, late at night, a presumably escaped show horse trotting past the outdoor cafés like a collective hallucination. But never any goats.

He fetched binoculars from a backpack. Scattered groups of them freckled the slopes, some lying down, other groups standing. There were black goats and brown goats and gray goats and cream-colored goats and goats harlequined with some or all these colors. Some goats were splotchy and some were bearded and others were shaggy and all of them, so far as Adi could tell, had horns that curved upright and back from their heads, like twinned scimitars. Adi expected the goats to peer back at him—he was an intruder, after all; at the very least, one would think, a curiosity—but possibly owing to the distance they seemed unaware or uninterested that he'd come ashore. After a while he waved and shouted but still they didn't notice or care. Adi lowered the binoculars, squinting. He couldn't help but read their indifference as either hubris or stupidity or some insolent combination of the two. They'd been ransacking this island for a century and a half and had no apparent concern that he was bringing it to an end.

Before that, though, Adi needed to tend to himself.

Entering the doorway of the beachside hut required ducking and once inside he had to hunch to keep his head from scraping. According to the foundation, long-ago sealers had built the hut, but Adi, crooked at the waist, was sensing the handiwork of dwarves. He rotated slowly, trying to fathom how anyone had ever existed here and at the same time how he was going to exist here for the next five weeks.

The hut was composed of a single small room, about twelve meters square, with slapdash-looking walls made of chinked logs and salvaged boards topped with a brittle thatched roof. Adi didn't know exactly when seal-hunting ended on the island but the cigarette butts on the floor and a pile of empty beer cans in one corner indicated someone had been here since. Though not very recently: the beer cans weren't aluminum but rather steel with oldfangled cone tops, relics from another era. Hanging on a wall was another relic, a framed black-and-white portrait of an old woman wearing pince-nez glasses and a lace bonnet. On her face was a withering frown, her mouth so downturned that it appeared incapable of an upturn, and Adi found himself pondering what comfort she could've possibly supplied and to whom she might've supplied it. The depth of that frown seemed intended to ward off not evil spirits but rather high ones.

Furnishing the hut was a single chair and two identical beds. The beds had webs of ropes like brawny fishing net strung between the rusted frame rails. Overlooking one of them was a window, or rather a crude opening in the wall that in its odd placement—not in the center of the wall but in a lower quadrant—hinted at a later renovation, perhaps a sealer's hand-sawn bid to escape his partner's stench or the relentless glower of his partner's mother. As a luxury it was slight, but still, because of it, Adi chose that bed for his own.

Bag by bag and box by box he moved himself into the hut. Nearly all of them had been packed by the foundation so each was a surprise for Adi to open, like some dour simulacrum of a birthday. He designated one corner of the hut the pantry and there assembled his cache of food: sacks of rice, lentils, and dried peas, all branded with the foundation's famine relief logo; powdered eggs and powdered milk, likewise branded; cans of mackerel and salmon; and a case of individually wrapped bars marked "E$_3$." Out of habit he glanced around for a discreet place to store the toilet paper before remembering he would have no visitors here. He stacked the rolls next to the doorway beside the small shiny shovel they'd packed him for burying his waste. He wasn't sure what the plastic bucket was for but he placed that near the doorway too.

Under the bed he slid a rudimentary tool kit—hammer, saw, pliers, a hand drill—and beside it, after a brief inventory, an unnervingly extensive medical kit. A situation requiring him to use all three of the provided tourniquets was both ghastly and difficult to imagine, especially since Adi had never been confident in his ability to use a tourniquet in the first place. With this darkening his mind, he lifted the satellite phone from its case and confirmed its full battery charge. This was his emergency lifeline, the foundation had told him, with the caveat that help was at best seven hours away. *So don't get hurt,* they'd told him, spoken as a punchline.

For a dresser he used the opposite bed, mounding the few items of clothing he'd brought himself beside the much larger tranche of clothing provided by the foundation—camouflage fatigues, mostly, although the foundation's firearms consultant had told him camouflage wouldn't be necessary, not at first anyway. It would be a while before the goats started perceiving him as a threat.

And here, lastly, on the floor, was the means of that threat. Bending from the chair Adi unlocked the rifle case and then, back upright, with his hands on his knees and his feet spread wide, sat staring at what it contained. *We're gonna set you up with a .308 bolt-action center-fire,* the firearms consultant had told him. *Titanium action, nice and light for scooting up and down those slopes.* The firearms consultant was a short muscly American woman wearing flip-flops and an oil company–branded cowboy hat. *Nice soft recoil so you won't feel hammered all day. We'll ship you out with 147-grain NATO rounds, German surplus, plus some 168-grain in a Barnes Triple Shock for when you need that extra knockdown. Goats are a little slab-sided but even with the NATO rounds you should be lethal out to three hundred yards.*

Adi lifted the rifle from its foam cushioning and laid it upon his knees. It was long and lean and somehow, like any perfected technology, like a spoon or a book, simultaneously elegant and crude. Its barrel was steel but blued so that it seemed to absorb rather than reflect light. On its gray carbon-fiber stock were squiggles of black paint that reminded Adi of the spirillum bacteria slides he used to make his science students examine under microscopes. He supposed the squiggles were a form of camouflage, designed to break up a visual pattern, but had there been anyone around, one of his nerdier students, he might've cracked wise about hunting germs.

He tipped the rifle over in his lap. On this side was the titanium bolt handle, which made a pleasing *cha-chick* when Adi slid it back, and then another, even more satisfying sound when he jammed the bolt forward and folded back the handle. With his thumb he softly rubbed the rifle's butt and forestock. He thought of lawmen and outlaws from books and movies who considered their weapon their best friend and thought he could understand, maybe, how this might happen. Having this thing that would kill for you. That could undo wrongs. This thing that wouldn't refuse your best and worst impulses.

Fastened to the rifle's top was a black scope resembling an elongated hourglass. Adi tried peeping through it, but with both his eyes open he found it difficult to see anything. A jumpy moon of visibility inside the otherwise black ambit kept jerking in concert with his head. By shutting his left eye, however, and shifting his right eye closer to the scope, Adi found he could see clearly—so very clearly, and with such distant precision, that when aiming it out the open doorway he might as well have been looking through a telescope. On the opposite side of the cove, what must have been five hundred meters away, he watched a crab scramble up a rock. He raised his head to look for it without the scope but without the scope the crab didn't exist.

From one of the ammunition crates Adi fetched a single bullet. Outside on the beach he wedged the rifle between his left arm and torso while fumbling the bullet into the chamber. *Cha-chick.* The rifle felt volatile now, as though he'd hooked voltage to it, had like Doctor Frankenstein shocked life into it. He raised the rifle and slowly swung the barrel back and forth, seeking a target through the scope. The crab was gone but then he didn't want to shoot a crab anyway. He finally fixed the scope on the open Pacific out beyond the twin rock formations marking Eremos Cove, at a circlet of blue sea and sky, the crosshairs intersecting just below the horizon. Aiming at the biggest thing in the world, it occurred to him, was certainly one way to pass a marksmanship test. Adi flicked off the safety. He inhaled, exhaled. He squeezed the trigger.

The bang it made and the echoes that followed sounded like the island fracturing. If the bullet made a splash, Adi didn't see it, because the moment he fired the rifle it kicked back at him, and the scope—pressed against Adi's forehead when he pulled the trigger—bashed him between his eyebrows, fast and pressurized like a hole punch machine.

Ears ringing, and with what felt like a fresh cleft in his forehead, Adi swiveled to see if the goats on the hillsides had spooked. They hadn't. Most remained lying down, sunning themselves, though a few more than earlier seemed to be looking in Adi's direction, with two or three craning their necks to see what the noise had been about.

Adi rubbed at the throbbing above his eye and was startled to see his fingertips glossed with blood. The scope had opened an arch-shaped gash and blood was leaking down the side of his nose. Wiping it with his finger he spun back toward the water, away from the staring goats, not wanting them to see him bleeding, not wanting them to know this was the first time he'd ever fired a gun.

Adi had anticipated a multitude of difficulties on Santa Flora. Firing a rifle without injuring himself hadn't been among them. Nor had sleeping.

But on his first night on the island he found sleep impossible. Hour after hour he tossed and sighed and flipped himself onto his left side then onto his right then onto his back. His grandmother had always advised counting sheep to fall asleep, but considering his present mission this felt mildly discordant; he'd be counting enough hoofed creatures in the coming weeks, not likely restfully. Insomnia had never plagued him before, not like this. Even in the rawest times— after his son died, after his wife left—he'd always managed to sleep. He tapped his fingers against his chest. He futzed with his pillow. He blinked in the pitch dark. Then at some muzzy point between midnight and dawn he concluded it was the silence keeping him awake.

It wasn't truly silence, by definition: he could hear

the cove lapping the beach and waves going *shoosh* against distant rocks and every now and again there'd come a bleat from the hills. But to Adi it was. To fall asleep in the capital—to fall asleep almost anywhere else on earth, he figured—was to drift off within an elaborate soundscape: not just car horns and sirens and televisions and neighbors and dogs but the lesser frequencies at which clocks tick and floors creak and refrigerators hum and drains purl and at twenty-five thousand feet jets go murmuring across the sky. Conjured by the capital's din, for Adi, was a sense of giant gears beneath the pavement that powered everything above, their constant turning like the beating of our hearts or the gurgling of our stomachs or the billowing of our lungs, invisible mechanisms that motor human existence and make civilization possible. Without those gears, without their screech and rumble and groan, life somehow felt, to Adi . . . unalive. Like the world was holding its breath.

He ventured outside twice to urinate. The first time, lifting his eyes to the night sky, he nearly splashed himself. Despite years of guiding his fourth graders through their astronomy block, and being familiar enough with the celestial charts to identify the major constellations, Adi had never encountered or even envisaged a sky like this one. Absent the smog and glow of the mainland, the view here contained almost more light than dark, more stars than sky. They were everywhere, a profusion of glints and pricks and silver glitter that extended all the way down to the horizon, as though a swarm of moths had descended upon the black fabric of the night and perforated it with an infinitude of holes. Still peeing, Adi tilted himself back to take in as broad a view as he could. Behind some of the star clusters were what looked like fumes of light, hazy cosmic vapors of purple and brown and blue, and not once but twice Adi watched a meteor slash the sky. The immensity of it all drew a gasp. No textbook or documentary had prepared him for this. He stood gaping up at it long after his bladder was drained, his back still arced, his mouth still open.

On his second trip outside there came a different jolt. It was barely dawn, the cove and its surrounding slopes veiled in a violet half-light and the gray sky seamed with stringy cloud formations as in a slab of marble. Adi came tottering out of the hut in his underwear to the edge of the water and was just about to pee when, glancing right, he saw them: one, two, three ... seven goats, standing in a crooked line by a thicket of mangroves and dwarf palms. Seven goats, staring at him.

Out of mannerly instinct he twirled away to cover

himself, and then, thinking that in his sleepless delirium he might've hallucinated the goats, pivoted slowly back around. But the goats were still there, all seven of them, still staring. Aside from their coloring, and their varying degrees of shagginess, Adi saw little to differentiate one from another. Their eyes were horizontally slitted, like sideways cat eyes, which made their expressions eerily vacant, even druggy. Some of them had long flowy beards, like the old men in Dr. Seuss books. One flared its nostrils in a dimly hostile way; another licked its lips; all kept their eyes trained on Adi. They were like a phalanx of soldiers, tensed, stone-faced, awaiting some order. Not quite consciously Adi raised his hands, stumbling back a few steps.

Or were they like soldiers? As with the dolphins leaping behind the boat to Santa Flora, Adi couldn't see any clear motive for their presence. Might they be an investigatory team, come to size up their island's newest citizen? Or could they be some sort of dreadfully awkward welcoming party? Or maybe an anti-welcoming party, assembled to intimidate the invader with the gun, to let him know they were on to him and his island-saving mission, maybe butt him with their horns, gore him into the sand? Adi dropped another step back.

Then he remembered that mission. He'd been hired to kill as many goats as he could, as quickly as he could. And here were seven of them. He shuffled backward to the hut, watching the goats watching him, then came out carrying the rifle, with five rounds loaded and two more bullets tucked into the waistband of his underwear.

Ten meters in front of the goats, he raised the rifle and clicked off the safety. And then, with a sigh, he lowered it. Something about this felt terribly wrong. The point-blank ease of it, maybe. The goats' ignorant, weird-eyed stares. The mean-spiritedness of slaughtering visitors to your doorstep.

Except, as he reminded himself: this wasn't sport hunting, with its contrived codes of conduct, or even war, with its similarly contrived conventions. This wasn't a contest. Fair play and fair chase didn't apply and neither did decorum. A shot to the head at close range, he thought, was no better or worse than one at long range. Bullet equaled bullet and dead equaled dead. He raised the rifle again and swung the barrel toward the goat farthest to the left, pinning the crosshairs just above its eyes. This was the job he'd taken. This was how Santa Flora would be saved. His fingertip stroked the trigger. Like the captain had said: *Killers kill.*

But again the rifle came slanting down. He'd failed to think things through, he realized. Shooting the goats would leave him with seven carcasses strewn across what was essentially his front sidewalk. Could he lift a dead goat? They must weigh eighty or ninety kilograms, he guessed. And where would he move them? He could roll or drag them into the cove, he supposed, but the cove was where he intended to swim and bathe, ideally absent rotting flesh. And might seven bleeding goat carcasses lure sharks into the cove? With the small shovel he had, he could conceivably bury them in the sand but digging seven graves with an oversized garden trowel might take him an entire day. Plus this little beach was where he cooked and ate his meals, where he intended to string up the hammock the foundation had packed him, where he planned to seek nightly refuge from the business of eradicating goats. The whole island would soon be their graveyard, that was true, but those graves needn't reach his front door.

He toggled the rifle's safety back on. The goats kept staring. One cocked its head, as though intrigued by this latest plot twist in the stirring drama Adi was performing for them. Adi felt himself begin to seethe. Here he was, a man with both the moral imperative and the means to slaughter these goats, and here they were smugly immunized against the danger he posed, as though in less than twenty-four hours they'd deciphered how to gather in the one tiny parcel of the island where he wouldn't dare shoot them, where instead he would entertain them with a dithering Hamlet act in his briefs. He raised the rifle again and swung the barrel from goat to goat, ferociously now, the way a robber holds up a bank.

Not a single goat flinched. The one on the left had ripped off a palm frond and was lazily chomping it, like a theatergoer with popcorn, and this, for Adi, was the final blow, the proof of their disdain.

Get out! he shouted, swinging the rifle at them. *Shoo!*

The head-cocking goat cocked its head again—this was, after all, yet another plot twist—while the chewer kept chewing.

Go! he yelled, lunging several steps toward them. *Leave! Go!*

The goats skittered back a bit, but only just a bit; to Adi they still appeared to be taking in the show. Adi could feel his face flushing, and a thatch of humiliation catching in his throat. He clicked off the safety, aimed the rifle skyward, and let off a round.

This did shake the goats, or at least shook the four

of them that went scooting sideways with their jaws slung open. For the remaining three, still staring, Adi fired a second round skyward. This sent the full lot of them skidding backward before they turned and fled in seven different directions.

Why Adi dropped the rifle and gave chase he didn't really know; what felt like a blast of dumb fury propelled him forward, barefooted and flush-faced, into the green thicket. He didn't make it very far. The sand was soggy here, a viscous tidal squish, and the mangrove roots were outspread in ankle-high hoops. A thick vine snared him by the armpit as he tried to windmill his way through the leafage, and from there, half-suspended on the looped vine, like an insect in a spider web, he watched the last of the goats go vanishing into the thicket with a measure of nimbleness and grace that he wouldn't have expected. The flick of their tails felt like a message Adi didn't need decoded.

Once he'd disentangled himself from the vine Adi slid his hands to his knees and stayed bent like that for a while, more winded than he ought to have been—though from frustration rather than exertion, from the humiliation still clogging his throat. Panting, he watched his toes being sucked into the caramel-colored goop, watched a red-tailed dragonfly lift off from a mangrove knee, and then, at the farthest edge of his vision, saw what looked like a brief and spasmodic flutter of wings.

Adi went to them. They belonged, indeed, to a bird: small and, at a cursory glance, rather plain-looking, with buff-colored feathers at its top and olive-brown feathers at its bottom. It looked to Adi, at first, like the sort of ordinary bird one sees in city parks, perching on the backs of benches or on the hat brims of statues. Lowering himself to his knees, however, Adi could see it wasn't quite that ordinary. Its tapered beak was long and curved, and, most strikingly, atop its head was a bristled shag of feathers that reminded Adi of the gel-spiked hair favored by the more avant-garde middle schoolers back in the capital. He tried drawing closer to it but the bird scuttled underneath some interlaced mangrove roots then tried flying out the opposite side. Adi watched it stumble and pitch sideways. Only one of its wings was flapping. The other was broken.

It wouldn't survive out here, Adi thought, not when the tide came in. So he reached under the roots and scooped the bird into his cupped hands. It was as light as an envelope. On the way back to his hut he felt its wing flutter against his palms and whispered for it to stay calm.

He scanned the hut for something in which to keep it, his eyes landing on the box marked "E3" that contained his nutrition bars. He tumped the box over with his foot to empty it and then carefully lowered the bird into the box. The bird peeped and hopped to a corner. Adi draped a T-shirt over the box while he went outside to gather some habitat for it: grasses, leaves, sticks, some handfuls of sand, a clamshell for fresh water ... he didn't know what else the bird might need. He didn't know what it ate, for instance. Or where it roosted or nested. Or just what variety of strange bird it might be.

Among the items the foundation had packed for him was a miniature library: a half dozen or so books and pamphlets about the island's history and ecology. *Some inspirational reading,* they'd told him, less clearly as a punchline. A translation of the seventeenth-century pirate William Dampier's *A New Voyage Round the World*. A photocopied article about Santa Flora bird life, in English, from a 1928 issue of *The Condor: A Magazine of Western Ornithology*. A ten-year-old United Nations subcommittee report entitled *A Biodiversity Strategy and Action Plan for Santa Flora*. But most important, for now, *A Field Guide to the Birds of the Central Pacific Ocean*.

Page by page, and picture by picture, Adi combed

the book for his bird, flipping through hundreds of photographs and illustrations. But none of the birds were his. Some looked similar. His seemed to have close cousins in the warbler family, yet none of the many species of warblers quite matched. None of them possessed that distinctively curved beak and that up-spiked crown.

Eventually Adi came to an appendix: "Extinct Birds of the Central Pacific Ocean." And there it was, his bird.

The Santa Flora Reed Warbler, first cataloged by a British ornithologist in 1876. *Last specimen seen, 1983.*

Oh shit, said Adi, peeling back the T-shirt to reexamine his bird, his eyes bouncing between the bird in the book and the bird in the box. *You're not supposed to be here.*

Its call, said the book, was chipped and shrill, sounding something like a squeaky wheel. Its long arced beak was for hunting insects on the ground, which was also where it nested. It had gone extinct, the book said, due to *habitat degradation from feral ungulates.*

From the goats. Adi looked up from the book. From the goats he'd just failed to kill. From the goats he'd spooked into the thicket, where (he feared) they'd trampled and smashed the wing of this tiny, delicate, ground-nesting bird that might or might not be the last of its kind.

Adi slumped. From the portrait on the wall the coal-colored eyes of the old woman felt to be singeing his chest. She looked no longer just disapproving but disgusted.

He lowered his gaze to the bird.

I'm sorry, he said to it.

The bird swiveled its neck to peer up at him.

I'll fix this, he said to it. *You'll see.*

The foundation's recommendation was to work the island as a grid, clearing the goats from one grid section before moving on to the next.

To that end, they'd supplied Adi with numerous maps. An absurd number of maps, really. One, annotated with Latin script, dated back to 1725 and depicted Santa Flora as an ear-shaped clod of pointy mountains and pointier trees. The objective of another, from 1829, seemed to be to flag prime seal-hunting grounds: Puntas Léon and Focas; Cala de Pájaros in the west; Islotes Negros off the southern shore. Still another, photocopied like the rest, issued from World War II, when the United States Navy erected a radar station on the island's north end in case the Panama Canal came under attack.

This glut of maps suggested, to Adi, the work of zealous interns overfulfilling their duties. He'd seen many such interns in the foundation's offices during his orientations: soft-faced young people aglow with conviction, abuzz with righteous purpose. But Adi didn't mind the glut; in fact he was grateful for it. He found the maps fascinating, mostly because decade after decade, century after century, they'd scarcely changed. Absent humans, he supposed, that's more or less what land does. There'd never been roads or harbors or settlements to label, nor canals or reservoirs to add, nor borders to adjust, jurisdictions to mark. Only the inlets and crags and spits and scarps of the island's naked body. The exceptions were the two camps—Langosta in the north, and Eremos, his own, on the southwestern end—that began appearing during the whaling and sealing eras: X's on some of the maps, like tiny scars.

The one Adi chose to work from was an official government survey map from thirty years earlier. He liked the way its topographical lines swirled and snaked like the skeleton of a psychedelic album cover. He traced a finger up the western coast, plotting his first route. A shoreline hike might be easier than heading overland across the island and slogging up and down its volcanic slopes, he figured, and might also provide him a better sense of the island's dimensions, the way a burglar cases a house from the outside. He'd walk for four hours, he decided, allotting himself equal time for his return. How much distance he'd cover would be up to the island, and to the goats.

He put on the camouflage fatigues and laced and tied his new boots. He slid a big machete into a belt sheath, in case a trail needed blazing. Into a nylon bandolier he slotted eighty bullets and then slung it across his chest. Five more bullets went into the rifle, *cha-chick*. And then, after checking on the bird and arranging the T-shirt canopy to ensure enough air was circulating for it, Adi stepped outside the hut, strapped the rifle to his shoulder, and, feeling never more strange, headed north.

From the beginning it was a grind. Merely exiting Eremos Cove meant tramping through the same dense, wet mangrove thicket that he'd chased the goats into, but with a higher tide. By the time he'd squelched his way through, his waterlogged boots felt heavy as sandbags.

Turning up the western coast, however, it became clear to him that his soggy feet would only be getting soggier. There was no soil to be seen, and very little sand: a few C-shaped pockets of beach here and there, some barely spacious enough for a single sunbather. What he would have to traverse, instead, was a shoreline of rubbly puzzle pieces of black and weather-browned basalt extending north as far as he could see, some mere cobbles and others so large they'd demand hand-over-hand climbing, all of them separated by the wash and froth of the tide. The only way forward was to hopscotch from rock to rock, like a frog negotiating lily pads, over pools and rivulets of churny seawater.

When the water was too wide Adi found himself wading with the rifle above his head, bracing himself against the surprising undertow. At other times he'd clamber up a boulder only to find a steep drop to the sea on the opposite side. He worried that around any bend he might find an impassable inlet or an unscalable boulder and be forced to turn back.

And he almost did turn back, early on, when between a seething stretch of ocean and a vertical ten-meter bluff lay just a narrow squiggle of pointed rocks, like the petrified cuspids of an ancient sea monster. With sea spray dousing him, and whenever possible with his palm against the jaggy cliff side for balance, Adi stretched from tooth to tooth and reminded himself that rogue waves—one of the more animating topics in the fourth-grade oceanography block—were strictly an open-water phenomenon. But then maybe it didn't matter. When the shoreline finally softened into gentler slopes, and Adi came upon a small curl of a beach where he could sit and rest, he realized that not a single centimeter of him was dry.

What he also realized was that he hadn't seen—and seemed unlikely to see—a single goat. He leaned his rifle against a rock and sat scanning the coastline. There was little here for goats, he supposed: rocks, salt water, treacherously slick footings, a million bright orange land crabs scurrying over every surface. Hardly anything worth nibbling here save a curious-looking shrub edging the rocks that had fleshy, waxy leaves and fan-shaped flowers and seemed to Adi vaguely alien, like something transplanted from an asteroid.

With nibbling in mind, he fetched from his shirt pocket one of the foundation's E3 bars, whatever they might be. He unwrapped it and grimaced. It was glossy and brown and flecked with what appeared to be some species of grain. The resemblance to a compressed turd was so revoltingly exact that he forced himself to pin his gaze on a particular cloud while chancing his first bite, as though to hoodwink his own senses. The complexity of the flavors was a surprise but not a pleasant one: sawdust, petroleum, liver, baby aspirin, ChapStick. In protest, a gush of saliva pooled under his tongue. He couldn't bring himself to mock or malign the E3 bar; its purpose, as he understood it, was famine relief. But neither could be bring himself to swallow it. He rose to his feet and hocked it into the sand.

Within seconds a pair of crabs scuttled to it from opposite angles, the faster of the two nabbing it with its claws and swifting it away. From schoolteacher instinct, to even things out, Adi pinched off another bit of the E3 bar and lobbed it to the losing crab. In what felt like an instant, however, the entire little beach was overrun with orange crabs, a scrambly profusion of life that swarmed so abruptly Adi found himself drawing back a few steps in alarm. When they continued mobbing toward him Adi clambered atop the rock and from there watched them teem. For a moment he felt like one of his country's former dictators, speechifying from a balcony, but as he started chucking morsel after morsel to the crabs, watching them scrabble and pile and skitter and claw, he felt more akin to a conductor steering an orchestra. To the woodwinds he pitched a tidbit then to the brass he tossed another—frenetically now, hamming it up—then to the strings another, and when the E3 bar was no more he raised his outspread arms as though to wrest a cadenza from his thousand-legged orchestra.

When the crabs began mounting his rock Adi grabbed his rifle and fled. Farther up the shore he stopped again, this time to check his map. As best he could determine, squinting at the whirly blue lines, he was roughly halfway up the western coast. From here the shoreline looked to be softening, the cliffs reclining into slopes, the basalt less rubbly and broken. In places it bulged into the sea in what looked like mammoth belly rolls. Here and there, as he walked, Adi encountered skimps of mosses and grasses, but the mosses were bedraggled and the grasses uneven, obviously bothered by teeth; he was entering the realm of the goats now, he sensed, testing the weight of the rifle on his shoulder.

Yet instead of goats, as he descended to the longest stretch of beach he'd encountered thus far, Adi found himself staring at something else: a giant heap of trash, most but not all of it the plastic variety. Hundreds of cloudy water bottles. A car tire. Beer cans, torn netting, bamboo sticks. A half-deflated pool float. Plastic bags, plastic lids, lengths of soggy rope. Styrofoam takeout trays, antifreeze jugs, a fat orange fishing buoy. All of it piled at one edge of the beach in such a way that Adi found himself scouting for a human culprit, as though behind a boulder a bulldozer might be hiding. What else could account for a man-high mound almost tidily amassed at this nook of rubbly shore? Adi stood frowning with his hands on his hips. The island was hundreds of kilometers from the mainland, an entire blue world away. Had passing ships been dumping their waste here, using Santa Flora as a garbage can? The netting said aye, Adi thought, the buoy seconding it.

But then—maybe not. He bent down to free a familiar-looking item from a plastic tangle, and turning it in his hands grunted softly. Maybe the trash had floated in on ocean currents and been tidied by the surf. Maybe it'd been bobbing in the Pacific for years before beaching here. He raised the item in his palm as though weighing it. It was a four-inch-tall Teenage Mutant Ninja Turtle action figure, the one with the purple bandanna, the one his son, Jairo, had loved most. The plastic was cracked and faded and coated with some sort of crusted sea slime but Adi slipped it into his pocket anyway, blew the air from his cheeks, and with a snap of his head moved on.

Farther north the coastline was carpeted in places with a rust-red shag of washed-up seagrass that sucked Adi's boots when he tried crossing it, the rotten tendrils stroking his pant legs like tentacles. In other places hairy green mosses extended to the water's edge, permanently damp from the sea spray, and the spongy feel of walking on them felt strange and somehow violating, like walking on actual hair. For these and other reasons Adi shifted his route upland, scaling a sheer black escarpment to where a wide tawny tableland stretched toward the island's center, here and there green with patches of thorny scrub. Surely, he thought, he'd find some goats here. He paused to look through the rifle scope, his crosshairs skating across the landscape.

But instead of goats, to his shock, he spotted a boat. It appeared to be a smallish boat—certainly smaller than the naval vessel that'd deposited Adi here—and it was sitting a ways offshore. Precisely how far offshore Adi couldn't gauge, but when he tried squinting at the boat without the scope he couldn't make out much beyond its white boaty shape.

With the scope, however, he could clearly see two men aboard. He felt himself scowling. The men's existence both surprised and disappointed him. Believing himself to be the only human for hundreds of kilometers in any direction had been an odd comfort and an odder source of pride. Encountering other humans, even at a distance, felt like discovering that his hotel room had been double booked and he'd be forced to share. It upended something. One of the men was bent over in the boat's stern hosing off multiples of something gray and glossy—fish, Adi guessed, their morning's catch. Santa Flora struck Adi as a prohibitively remote place to fish, a distant haul from any port, but then what did he know. He vaguely recalled the naval captain mentioning something about fishing boats. *Nasty bastards*, he remembered now: that'd been his phrase. Maybe some of the trash heap was owing to them.

He lowered the rifle and returned his gaze landward, and that's when he saw it. The pale head of a goat poking out from one of the green scrub brakes. Immediately Adi dropped to his knees and shimmied behind a rock. Through the scope he watched the goat tearing off leaves and sometimes dipping its head so that only the tips of its horns were visible, like a pair of shark fins. As with the fishing boat, Adi wasn't sure how to gauge the goat's distance from him. Back in the capital, distances were measured by city blocks or bus stops but here there were neither. The foundation's firearms consultant had told him his shots would be reliable out to three hundred yards, which was more or less three hundred meters, which was more or less three football fields. But Adi found it impossible to multiply football fields in his mind's eye, to lay them end to end like train cars. He decided to move closer.

Stalking didn't come naturally to him. For a model he relied on the cops and commandos he'd seen in movies, twirling around corners, belly-wriggling under fire. He crept low from bush to bush and from stone to stone, one eye always pinned to the goat, which seemed oblivious—or maybe indifferent—to his lurching approach.

Eventually he made it to a zigzaggy row of waist-high volcanic cinders uphill from the goat. Behind the largest of these, to compose himself, he lay on his back for a moment with his eyes clasped shut, the midday sun blazing his face. Adrenaline was shuddering him, his breath coming in gasps. It did not escape him that he was engaged in one of humankind's most elemental practices, the stuff of prehistory, of spears and loincloths. His ancestors had enacted this very same dance, in era after era and on any number of continents, apparently with success because here he was. Yet an honest accounting of that lineage, he thought, would need to exclude his father, who'd worked behind a jewelry counter all his life, and his grandfather, a revolutionary turned professor of mathematics. Only the latter might have ever held a weapon, and if he'd ever fired it it had been at other men. If there remained any genetic memory for Adi to retrieve it was surely sunken and decayed. He was on his own.

He rolled over and with the rifle's barrel resting on the rock watched the goat through the scope. It was definitely less than a football field away from him, probably midfield to goal. Because of the scrubby cover surrounding the goat Adi didn't have a clear view of its trunk so, not without qualms, he figured he would have to try for a more difficult head shot. He pegged the scope's crosshairs above where the goat's jaws were mashing leaves, just behind its eye, trying to ignore the thudding of his heart.

He touched off a shot. For several seconds, following the rifle crack, all the world seemed flash frozen— including the goat, which was standing as upright as before. It'd stopped its chewing and was now glancing casually uphill. After a moment, with what Adi interpreted as a blithe shrug, it lowered its head and went back to eating.

He'd missed. Of course he'd missed. After the debacle with the scope smacking his eye socket he'd set up a makeshift rifle range but hitting the target even half the time was still an accomplishment for him. For his second shot he moved the crosshairs to the goat's chest, or rather where beneath the scrubby green cover he thought the goat's chest would be. Aiming for the lungs, he remembered the firearms consultant advising, was the best means of both ensuring a kill shot and conserving ammo. This time he held his breath to keep the crosshairs from jiggling and when he couldn't hold his breath any longer he squeezed the trigger.

Again, as the rifle crack went echoing across the island, the world froze. But the goat, when Adi glanced over the scope, was no longer part of that world. It'd dropped out of sight. *Oh God,* he said aloud, flooding with horror and regret and a peculiar kind of fear, the rifle suddenly trembling in his hands. *Oh God,* he said again. He scrambled to his feet and came around the cinder pointing the barrel at where just seconds ago the goat had been feeding. One of the bushes moved sideways, as if kicked or jostled from below, then went still. With the rifle's buttstock pressed tight into his shoulder Adi walked slowly down toward it, choking back a despondent moan that felt even more elemental than what he'd just done, residuum from pre-prehistory, from bloodless Eden. *Oh God,* he said again.

The goat was already dead when he got to it, a bright red hole in its side where the mushrooming bullet had, in an instant, blown apart its heart. It was owing to dumb luck, Adi knew, but his shot had been remarkably true. For a long while he stood over the dead goat, his chest heaving, mouth open, his eyes barely blinking. He'd never killed anything before—

nothing larger or more sentient than an insect, or rather a mouse if you counted the traps he'd occasionally set in the family's apartment—but the initial horror of it was giving way to a more complex field of emotions that he found difficult to sort. His revulsion diluted by some old-stone savage pride at the cleanliness of the kill. His sadness tempered by relief that he was capable of carrying out the mission he'd accepted.

The battle to save Santa Flora, he realized, had officially begun. He'd just fired its first shots, clocked its first casualty. Pooling below the flattened scrub was its first spilled blood.

He laid the rifle uphill of the goat and sat down on his heels. Only after the goat's eyes had skinned over did he muster the nerve to touch it, gingerly resting his palm upon its haunch. But the flesh felt so warm and pliant and undead that with a jump Adi's hand recoiled from it, and in doing so he jerked its leg enough to expose clean pink teats on its belly. He'd shot a female, a nanny goat. He wrapped his arms around his knees and, angling away from the goat, began rocking on his heels. *I'm sorry,* he whispered.

But Adi wasn't sure if that was true, or wholly true. And for a terribly long time, until the sun was tilting westward, he rocked beside the carcass trying to figure out if it was. At one point, raising his head, he noticed that the fishing boat was still anchored offshore and he found himself wondering, passingly, if one of the fishermen he'd watched earlier might be doing the same thing as he was now, sitting next to what he'd slain, trying to fathom what in God's name he'd done.

Carrying the carcass back to Eremos Cove had never, for a moment, been part of Adi's plan.

But rising to leave the goat he felt himself queerly restrained, as though held fast by a magnet. What would become of it now? There were no rodents or other mammals on Santa Flora to scavenge the carcass, no condors or vultures either. Surely there were flies on the island though Adi had yet to notice any, even at his latrine, and he didn't know what other insects, if any, might be drawn to the carcass.

With the toe of his boot Adi nudged the goat's shoulder. Santa Flora seemed poorly equipped for the cycle of life that he used to teach his fourth graders about—death, decay, rebirth, the dying of one organism nurturing the living of another—at least as that cycle pertained to the island's occupier goats. The island was never meant to accommodate them: not in life, clearly, but likewise not in death. He feared the goat would just lie here, unpicked, undesired, unredeemed, until at some distant point its bones would flake into the ashy soil as a superfluous and pointless seep of fertilizer.

But then what had he expected? He'd been hired to save the island by ridding it of goats: the live ones, not the dead. *It's not easy work but it's noble work*, his interviewer had said. So again Adi tried walking away from it, re-shouldering his rifle and restarting downhill. But again he came up short. This time, however, he was able to identify the magnetic pull. Killing the goat had been one thing; killing it and abandoning it, as though it was worthless litter, a banana peel, a mango seed, the trash heap back on the beach, felt like another.

The goat needed to feed something. Even the ancients, he reminded himself, ate their sacrifices. The goat needed to feed something and absent anything else that something would have to be Adi.

Bending forward, then, he grabbed the dead goat by its hooves and with much stumbling and grunting heaved it onto his shoulders to begin the long march home.

From the first few steps he sensed he wouldn't make it, not like this. The carcass was heavy—maybe seventy kilograms, he guessed, not that far from his own weight—so staying upright required him to stagger along with an awkward forward hunch, difficult uphill and almost impossible down. Every step drew a pained croak. By the time he made it to the escarpment—his route back to the shoreline and, steep and slick, another problem in itself—his leg muscles were seething and his ankles threatening to buckle. At the top of the escarpment he let the goat slide off his back and for several minutes stood there motionless, facing the ocean with his eyes shut, until his heart rate slowed closer to the breaking of the waves below.

What struck him, when at last he opened his eyes, was the sight of the fishing boat. Had the fishermen been watching him this whole time, as he went floundering toward the coastline with a blood-stained goat around his shoulders? He imagined them passing a pair of binoculars back and forth, frowning, then shrugging, and felt pitted with embarrassment.

His more immediate problem, however, was getting the carcass down the near-vertical scarp, from the height of a second-story window. Climbing up it hadn't been difficult, with its rocky juts and sockets, and descending wouldn't be that hard either—unless you were ferrying a dead goat. He imagined the fishermen laughing at him, *what's the crazy fool going to do now?* The goat was far too heavy to carry or drag with one hand, the scarp way too steep for him to try navigating without his hands, and he lacked any rope with which to lower it. He could think of nothing else to do but to tip it over the edge.

Just seconds after doing so Adi flung his spread hands up to block his own view. The goat rolled a couple of times before clipping a rock outcrop and bouncing, gravity whirling its legs outward and then, with an audible snap, gravity breaking them when the goat hit another ledge, until with a gruesome gassy thud the carcass came to rest half in the water and half on a craggy black boulder, its forelegs splayed in terribly wrong directions. The fall must've ruptured something inside the goat, too, because when Adi got down to it he saw bluish-purplish blood bubbling from its mouth. *I'm sorry,* he said to it again. *God, I'm sorry.*

He made sure not to glance toward the fishing boat as he worked the goat back onto his shoulders. And he spun quickly out of view when the goat's sphincter muscle went limp and a spate of oval brown pellets went tumbling down his shirt, fast as coins from a change machine. But scarcely a minute later he felt certain he could hear the fishermen cackling at him when, struggling to maneuver the goat's weight over damp wet mossy rocks, he slid it off his back again, onto a green shag of sea moss, and choking back a defeated sob dropped his hands to his knees.

Ah ha, it's too heavy for the fool, he imagined the fishermen saying, correctly. It was too heavy by half. The sun would be setting soon. He'd never make it like this.

What he needed, Adi thought, was some way to lighten the load, his fingers skimming the big machete in his belt sheath. Was that even possible, using a blade meant for whacking brush and vines? He didn't know. In his life, animal flesh had always appeared wrapped in cellophane, and like everyone else he'd avoided considering how. He slipped the machete out of its sheath and brushed its long blade across the goat's matted hair. The legs were his handles for carrying the carcass—Adi didn't think he could lose those. The only parts that really seemed expendable were the goat's head and neck. He raised the machete high, wincing at his likeness to an executioner. *I'm sorry,* he said again, and then brought the blade down.

The way the goat's face animated when the machete struck its neck—the harrowingly living way that its eyes bulged and lips flared—drew from Adi a long honking sob that felt wrenched from his subconscious, as though the blade had also rent some obscure pocket of innocence within him. He knew the goat's reaction was from the machete forcing dead air up its trachea but, insensate or not, what he'd witnessed, and induced, was an anguished grimace. When his breathing steadied Adi swung the blade again, desperate to get this over with, but his second strike only managed to open a parallel maroon gash in the goat's neck.

On his fifth and hardest swing Adi hit bone; tiny ivory shards glistened on the blade edge. He paused to wipe his forearm across his eyes to clear them of the tears glossing his cheeks. He went down to his knees and switched from swinging with two hands to one, every other chop punctuated by a deeper and throatier sob, hack after hack mauling the goat's flesh into draggled purple fibers and splintering the vertebrae and bloodstaining the sea moss until finally the neck and head came free from the withers.

Adi reeled back from the carcass, still on his knees, and with his shirtsleeve smeared together the sweat and snot and tears and spatters of blood on his face. What he was doing was right, he told himself. His blurred gaze found the fishing boat. His chest heaved. Everything he was doing was right.

Twenty or thirty minutes down the coastline, when the horror and adrenaline wore off, it became plain to him that beheading the goat had lightened it only fractionally. With the sun nearing the horizon, attended by yellowing clouds, Adi was still sagging under its weight.

Just south of the trash-heaped beach, then, he set the carcass down in a tidal slick where frothy white bands of foam were curling toward the sea. This time he worked methodically, without tears, using the machete to slice off the rear legs not unlike the way one breaks down a roasting chicken. These he kept. What remained of the carcass he towed into the surf until he'd waded well beyond the sandbar, to where the ocean was lapping his blood-drenched shoulders, and there he let it sink. He consoled himself with visions of small reef fish nibbling it down, or of a passing shark exhilarating at its gory good fortune. Back on land he grasped the rear legs by their hocks and, as though carrying two suitcases, resumed hiking southward.

But even this proved too much. The day's light withered into a deep indigo haze and nightfall began blackening the rock-strewn course he had to negotiate. He'd neglected to pack a flashlight, never imagining he'd be out after dark. Moving blindly from rock to rock was dicey, especially with moss and lichen slicking so many of them. More than once he slipped backward. The goat legs helped cushion a couple of those falls, and seawater others, but on one fall Adi smacked the back of his head on a rock. Tasting his fingertip in the dark, to check if he was bleeding, he realized the test was in vain. His blood, the goat's blood: if there was any difference he doubted he could taste it or for that matter do anything about it.

What was clear, however, was that he needed at least one free hand to make it back. So from atop a giant wedge of basalt Adi hurled one of the goat legs into the water, the final installment in his sacrifice to the sea, and then, for another two hours, he dragged the remaining goat leg behind him to Eremos Cove.

Emerging from the mangrove thicket he dumped the leg in the sand and made straight for his pallet of water. Bottle after plastic bottle fell to the beach as Adi guzzled them, another trash heap in its infancy. He slung off his wet bloody clothing and, with slightly less struggle than his first time doing so, got a fire going.

At the water's edge he stood the goat leg upright so that the cove lapped the bottom of the ham and with the machete he sliced off the skin and hair in rough moon-colored strips that got licked then swallowed by the waves. He didn't know precisely what he was doing but the process seemed intuitive if not maybe instinctual. From the thickest part of the leg he carved out a half dozen ribbons of purplish meat that he rinsed in the salt water before skewering them onto the machete blade.

Among his pantry staples were salt and pepper but Adi was too exhausted to bother. He sat beside the fire turning the blade in the flames, watching the meat sizzle and char and smoke and curl. Upon his face, in the wobbly bronze firelight, there was no expression. Despite the drifting smoke he barely even blinked.

Only when he drew the first hot strip of goat from the blade and bit into it, the inside lukewarm and raw and the exterior tough and reechy—only then did Adi come apart again. Only then did the tears resume.

He'd eaten meat all his life, save for a brief spell after college living with a vegetarian girlfriend, but he'd never tasted death before. Never before had he detected the flavor of violence on his tongue, the burnt taste of fear. Never before had he apprehended the stillness in his mouth, the inertness of muscle that'd once stretched and pulsed and twitched on a creature that'd nursed and played and cried and in its final moments kicked at the grass as though to outrun whatever was thieving its existence. Inside every sandwich he'd ever eaten had been that contraband. Dotting every pizza had been death.

Adi drooped the blade back into the fire and

rocked on his heels as sparks and meat smoke gyred around him. And then slowly, piece by piece, he ate the rest of it, sometimes chewing and crying at the same time, licking death from his fingers while telling himself, over and over again, that everything he was doing, all of it, was right.

Once, when Adi was a child, he asked his grandfather how he'd survived the darkest hours of the revolution, when starving people ate their horses and then their pets and then finally the rats feeding on the corpses of those who'd had neither horses nor pets. His grandfather's answer came so quickly it felt cursory: *If you've done something once you can do it forever,* he said. *Only the first time is difficult.*

Adi didn't know if this was true or not. Men of his grandfather's generation tended to shrug off past privations as a way (Adi suspected) of asserting superiority over their softer, more complacent descendants. But it might be true, Adi thought. And if it was, then killing the next goat, and the one after it, should be easier.

Still, he procrastinated. His reluctance to rise from bed Adi blamed, not unjustly, on his aching muscles. Every one of his body's fibers felt afflicted: those of his thighs and calves, from scaling the sea rocks;

his neck and shoulders, from portaging the carcass; and his lower back, from his multiple falls into the boulder-spiked surf. His head throbbed as well from where he'd smacked it on one of those falls; rubbing it, he could feel a crust of dried blood in his hair. He spent the morning sagging in and out of comfortless sleep. A triangle of sunlight was already advancing up the wall before he mustered the groany strength to sit up.

Once out of bed he trudged naked into the cove to bathe, scrubbing away all the mud and salt and blood and ash in rays of light so clear and white as to be antiseptic. Then for half an hour or longer he floated almost motionlessly on his back, trying to empty his mind into the seawater as the sunlight crisped his face. This slackness was good for him, he told himself. Therapeutic, he told himself. Necessary.

When at last he tilted himself upright and fluttered open his eyes he found himself facing the hillside with its distant scatters of goats. Despite all that'd happened yesterday, the goats appeared no fewer and no different than before: unaffected, undisturbed, undismayed. Were they not aware, Adi wondered, of what he'd done yesterday, of his swivel-eyed midnight sacrifice, of their sister's haunch roasted on a knife blade, or were they instead unbothered, possibly even relieved, because it hadn't been their back leg dripping into the flames?

On the way back to his hut Adi passed the firepit where half buried in the embers lay the blackened femur and tibia he'd been gnawing in last night's firelight.

He paused there, turning to squint up at the goats.

Had they caught the smell of it in the dark, he wondered, raised their noses to it, sniffed drowsily, blinked: the very exotic aroma of fire on Santa Flora, of course, but atop that smoky breeze something else besides: a charry bestial scent that was almost but not quite familiar, rather a distortion of the familiar, a perversion of it, an odor unidentifiable but unnerving all the same, a peculiar incense upon which floated terrible forebodings. When the conquistadors blitzed his country, Adi knew, they'd sometimes burned the natives alive. The stench was said to linger for days, even weeks. But had it really been the stench lingering, Adi thought now, gauging the air, or had it been the residual horror and fear? And just how greatly did the smell of scorched human flesh, he found himself thinking, before shaking the question from his head, differ from that of goat?

Back inside the hut he fed himself breakfast and then fed, or tried to feed, the bird he'd started calling E3, after the logo on its box. Unlike the crabs, but very much like Adi, the bird didn't seem fond of its namesake nutrition bars, which Adi had been crumbling into the box. Santa Flora Reed Warblers were known—had been known, before they'd gone extinct—to live on insects, not seeds, and certainly not individually wrapped, seed-flecked turd replicas. The bird watched flatly as Adi broke off fragments to add to an untouched pile in the center of the box, beside its clamshell of water. *I don't have any bugs,* Adi said to it after a while. *How would I get you bugs?* The bird lowered its head as though sensing its fate sealing.

What Adi did possess, he realized, was raw protein: goat meat, not insect meat, but meat all the same. At the edge of the cove he gathered up a few of last night's butchering scraps, rinsed the sand off them, and then, using a folding knife and a smooth level stone, minced them into what he gauged were beak-sized morsels.

The way E3 tore into them was both delightful and vaguely unsettling. *There there,* Adi said to the bird. *There's plenty for you,* laughing, *slow down.* The bird stabbed the meat with its beak, long and curved and pale like a sliver of moon, devouring the first five bits Adi gave it and then stepping back, fluffing its working wing, and eating a second helping of six more purple morsels. Adi smiled as he rained more goat bits into the box. *Vengeance must taste good,* he said to the bird. His students' faces had always squirreled when he'd tell them that dinosaurs' closest surviving relations were birds. Adi wished they could see what he was seeing now: fiercely living proof, a T. rex in miniature.

But also a reminder, it struck him, of the mission awaiting him outside. E3 needed more meat and Santa Flora needed fewer goats.

On went the damp stained camouflage fatigues, then, along with the still-squishy boots. Into the rifle went five bullets, *cha-chick,* and onto his shoulder went the rifle. And into the mangrove thicket, again, went Adi, this time headed east—inland—to see if his grandfather might've been right: that the first time was the only time that mattered.

Navigating dry land, once he was free of the mangroves, was a welcome change from the day before; hiking constantly uphill, however, was not. The capital, where he'd lived all his life, stood at sea level, its streets and sidewalks flat as a chessboard. But here, between the mighty escarpments, there were only slopes and slants, a jagged world atilt, and it wasn't long before Adi's breath was coming in chesty gasps and his sapped legs were threatening to buckle. He'd understood, in some nominal way, the link between goats and elevation, how goats excelled at navigating heights, how they preferred looking down to looking up, but his current route in search of them was hardly nominal or abstract; it was thrashing him. In a narrow chute of rubble, canted upward between boulders, Adi took advantage of some shade to let his heart cool. He wiped the sweat from his eyes, wondering, acidly, if he should expect to spend the next five weeks alternating between huffing and puffing.

Not long after, though, he came upon some goats. Five in one uphill group, and, more distantly, three more in another. Despite him ducking behind a boulder, whatever was about to happen wouldn't be an ambush. From their perch above him several of the goats were dully monitoring Adi's approach. They stared at him darting from one boulder to another in the leaden way people stare at televisions in waiting rooms before the goats returned to more interesting matters, such as the last scraggly shoots of a bush that a trio of them was nibbling bare. Once confident he was being ignored, Adi veered off to the south and then up a craggy incline to a position roughly level with the larger group, about forty meters out. There he tucked himself behind a rock shelf, propped his rifle upon it, and peered through the scope.

The goat closest to him, in the group of five, was shaggy and big-shouldered and sour-faced, an inviting target, but while Adi was flicking off the safety and steadying his shoulder the goat turned so that its tail was facing him. Not wanting to risk shooting it in the hindquarters, Adi slid the crosshairs to the right, to where another goat was standing, this one broadside. But this goat was considerably smaller than the others, its pelt short and tidy-looking and its recurved horns like little Arab daggers: a kid, Adi guessed, or a yearling, his fingertip backing off the trigger. He understood this particular crucible was inevitable—eradication meant the young and the old and every goat in between—but it needn't come today, he decided. Not for his first shot, anyway. He had three more goats to choose from.

Gliding the crosshairs back to the left he found two goats standing beside one another. Or rather something more than beside: The smaller of the two was nestled into the side of the other, like a spooning couple, and its eyes were closed, Adi couldn't help noticing, as though sedated by contentment or protection. He sighed, his fingertip detaching itself once again from the trigger. The last goat in the group, he saw, was lying down on the far side of the crescented pair, beneath the shield of their attachment.

None of this mattered, Adi scolded himself. Not the imperfect shooting angles nor the age of the goats nor whatever kindred affection, real or projected, was on display. His job was to shoot all of them, or at least as many of them as he could shoot before they fled. Whichever goat he chose to shoot first was meaningless: every one of them was an identical ecological toxin, cancer cells that bleated. There was no moral calculus to the selection, then, no principle that could slot one goat in front of another in the rifle queue—only sentiment. Nothing he was feeling could possibly matter.

Yet something about it *must've* mattered, to some part of him, because here he was, revisiting each goat with the crosshairs and each time finding his heart rate spiking and his fingertip paralyzed. It occurred to him how much easier it'd be if the foundation had equipped him with a machine gun rather than a bolt-action rifle. That way he could mow them down almost simultaneously, targeting not five individuals but rather an insentient blur of invasive hair and invasive horns and invasive hooves. That way he wouldn't have to think or choose.

But Adi had no machine gun. He did have to choose.

He recalled the old saw about throwing a dart at a

map, which felt almost too literal here: the five goats arrayed like five continents, his 147-grain dart brass-cased and lead-cored and chambered in the rifle. Too literal, and in some way, he thought, so glib in this context as to be depraved. If no order was articulable, then randomness was all there could be, fate as a dice roll. But what did that make Adi himself, crouched now behind his rifle—a mere instrument of dumb chance? Did it make him the hand or the dice? Could there truly be no reason—not one—that one goat would die this morning while tonight another would watch the sun set behind the ocean? Was there really no reason—not one—that his son Jairo was dead while everyone else's sons were still alive?

Adi yanked his head away and looked westward, to where blue met blue on the horizon. When finally he looked back the big sour-faced goat had turned broadside again. But it was too late. He ticked the safety back on and rose from behind the rock to his feet. The goats all turned to watch him, even the nestled one, all five craning their necks toward him and staring at him in silence. They stayed like this for a long time, frozen, and might've stayed that way forever had the smallest goat not bleated, drawing their attention away from Adi. Most of their attentions, anyway: the big goat still stared, indecipherably as always, though with just enough brassiness to make Adi feel he was being expelled. He slipped behind some boulders and, with his shoulders slumped, began hiking back home.

He hadn't gone far, however, before he chanced upon another goat. This one was by itself, and plainly a billy goat. Its horns, as thick as Adi's wrists at their base, rose up and out from its head like the wings of a flying raptor, and its coat was shaggy to the point of gross dishevelment, matted with twigs and leaf litter and thorny shoots. Most striking by far, however, was the odor: a musky pungent reek that called to mind rotting patchouli plus the urinal troughs in the capital's bus terminal plus yeasty gym socks abandoned for the summer in middle school lockers. The stench came drifting downwind to where Adi was standing, despite what seemed to him a safe distance. He wheeled away from the goat, folding an arm into his face, suffocating himself with his bicep against the odor's heavy creep.

When at last Adi turned back around, inhaling as shallowly and seldomly as he could while peering at the billy goat over his elbow, a deep, lopsided frown began wrinkling his forehead.

What the billy goat was doing was at first unclear. Adi thought it might be cleaning itself, a mild irony considering its stench and scraggliness. But it soon became clear that cleanliness wasn't its goal.

With its neck bent downward and back, and with a dazed, doped look in its one visible eye, the billy goat was suckling the end of its penis—bright pink and narrow and straight as a candle—its back legs shuddering gently at first then more violently as it continued. After a while, its whole body juddered and swayed and Adi flinched and grimaced as a spurt of semen glazed its beard. The billy goat threw its head up, with a spaced-out look of ravishment, and then, to Adi's even deeper shock, swiveled its neck back downward and went right back to slobbering itself, as though caught in an incontinent loop.

This couldn't be normal behavior, Adi thought. This had to be deviant. The goat must be sick in the head, tormented by some malignant hormonal imbalance, sex-deranged, a stanky slovenly pervert most likely out here alone because it'd been banished from the herd. Adi glanced away, cringing, feeling his grip tightening on the rifle stock. The sick goat was a hazard not just to the island but to its fellow goats as well.

His first shot clipped its neck. His second struck just above and behind its jaw. After the billy goat dropped Adi fired two more shots into its head then one into its chest until he was certain its lungs were finished pumping and then he stood there feeling his own lungs filling and unfilling and filling and unfilling and filling and unfilling.

This time he didn't run to the carcass. In fact he didn't go to it at all. Its meat wasn't fit for E3 and certainly not for himself. But Adi didn't take another shot that day. One kill felt like enough to prove, or at least suggest, that his grandfather had been right after all.

Adi woke the next morning with a revised plan for Santa Flora. It wasn't necessary to eradicate *all* the goats from the island, he decided. Only the males needed culling. Without billies, and therefore without kids, the nanny goats could live out their days in abbey-like peace until, one by one, as fresh green shoots began poking from the soil, they'd vanish quietly and serenely from the island. He was surprised that the foundation hadn't come up with this idea, if just for the efficiency of it alone; it sliced his labor roughly in half. Adi allowed himself a rare bout of immodesty. His plan felt close to brilliant.

Released from the pressures of wholesale shooting, then, from the now obsolete demands to notch an indiscriminate kill count, Adi decided to spend the day scouting the island from south to north then back again: billy goat reconnaissance, he told himself.

He spread his map on the bed and studied it while sipping famine-relief instant coffee, on occasion scattering flecks of dried goat meat into E3's box. From top to bottom Santa Flora stretched roughly sixteen kilometers, excluding its long comma tail, but that measurement wasn't overland distance—rather as a bird flew.

And we don't fly, do we, Adi said to E3, the bird drooping its head and hopping toward the salvaged Teenage Mutant Ninja Turtle Adi had placed in its box, as though to commiserate. Ninja Turtles couldn't fly either.

Where Adi and the bird and the Ninja Turtle were, Eremos Cove, was a small blue dent at the southwestern end of the island. Campo Langosta, Santa Flora's only other anchorage, sat on a slender neck of land at the northeastern end. Some variety of structure appeared to be there, possibly a sealers' hut like his own; on the topographical map was a tiny square mirroring the tiny square he and E3 were presently occupying. Between these squares on the map, however, was whorl after whorl of elevation, like a coloring book version of a Van Gogh nightscape, the swirled lines denoting cliffs and crags and wide banks of loose tuff cobbles. Between these squares was a grueling slog.

Bisecting the island's mountainous spine, however, was some kind of narrow valley or channel—a potential passageway from west to east about halfway up the island where some blue pools of water appeared strung like beads. The western coastline, as Adi had discovered on his first exploration, was a miserable snarl of wet basalt hunks and wetter surf. But the northeastern shore looked mellower—on the map, anyway; if he was reading it right, that is—with terrain that looked to slope toward the sea rather than collapse into it.

With his fingertip Adi traced a route. The arduous part would come early, when he'd need to negotiate the spinal ridgelines diagonally—to dodge the western shoreline but to also avoid a full-on transversal of the range. Yesterday had served up a hot spoonful of the kind of climbing required; today would serve up a bowlful. Still, relief should arrive when he'd descend into the valley pass and follow it to the eastern coast, where he'd turn north, hiking past Punta Este, Punta Léon, and Punta Focas before staggering—after dark, surely; wrecked, possibly—into Campo Langosta, whatever it might be.

To that end, he'd need a much fuller kit of gear than he'd been heretofore packing: headlamp, batteries, food, water...what else? Should he bring an extra set of clothes? He wasn't sure—maybe dry socks and underwear at least. What about toilet paper or his first aid kit or his spool of nylon rope in case the climbing got dicey? He deliberated over the heavy, clunky satellite phone as well, weighing it in his palm while amassing a host of imagined emergencies in his other palm before dismantling his mental balance scale and setting the phone back down.

The rifle was the final packing question. Adi was inclined to leave it; it made climbing more difficult, for one thing, but he was also envisioning this day as a reprieve from gunfire, as a reconnoitering exercise and nothing else. It occurred to him, though, that he might possibly come across another demented billy, or worse yet an appalling circle jerk of them. The mission was the mission, he told himself, swinging the rifle over his shoulder with a sigh.

About an hour into the hike, which was taking him past goat after goat after goat, Adi started counting them. By midday, when he stopped to eat a tin of salmon, he'd counted 313. They tended to congregate, he was beginning to notice, in groups of four or five, and almost always segregated by sex in much the same way his former fourth graders gathered during recess: the nannies over here, the billies there. Rarely did any of the goats react to Adi's approach—mostly they just craned their necks to watch him—and even then only when he was within thirty meters or so, close enough to see the flora gobbed between their teeth. He'd expected goats to cluster together in the face of danger, in the same way he'd taught his students that herd animals on the African savanna do when a lion is afoot, but instead the goats scattered toward higher ground, fanning out in multiple directions as though to brake any predator with the tyranny of choice. *Off duty,* he said to a solitary billy as he passed, gesturing to the rifle on his shoulder, *you're safe today.* The billy paused to gawp at him before stripping a saltbush branch into its mouth.

The next billy he came upon was dead. It was lying crumpled on a slope of lava rock about fifty meters up from Adi. Out of curiosity, he detoured to it. It'd been dead a long while, he gathered, steeling himself for an odor but finding none—long enough for what was left of its skin to be crisp and thin like parchment, for its flan-colored bones to be here and there exposed, and for what little remained of its baked white hair to be riddled with spiky moths. Yet what piqued Adi's interest were its horns: long and recurved and almost elegantly banded but most of all strangely vibrant despite the moldered shell of the rest of the goat, as though these twin decorative protrusions were exempt from the binaries of life and death. Crouching down to touch one, he swore he felt an impossible thrumming, the very faintest of vibrations like that of a piano string not quite done stirring after the note has faded from the hall. Applying the slightest pressure caused the horn to droop loosely into his hand, and with scarcely a tug Adi found himself sliding it off the skull. He rose to his feet turning the hollow horn in his hands, marveling at a gracefulness—an artfulness, even—that he hadn't registered before, not when such horns were fastened to musky and matted bucks. He slipped it into his backpack and moved on.

His climbing skills were improving, or else his legs were strengthening, or maybe he'd misread the topographic whorls that'd buffeted him with dread; whatever the reason, he found the going less strenuous than he'd feared. It helped that the day was mostly overcast, huge ratty meringues of cumulus drifting eastward across the sky and blessing Adi's paths with cool shadows. The paths themselves were never quite clear—at best, rude covert trails from ledge to ledge that he came to realize the goats had blazed. More than once it crossed his mind that he might've been the first human to negotiate some of those ledges, at least in spots—that from very narrow and particular angles he might as well have been Balboa or Magellan beholding virgin landscapes, with a not dissimilar mandate, he recognized, to alter them.

By mid-afternoon he reached the descent into the pass, the treeless crags spilling into a breach so green and misted that Adi found himself gaping down open-mouthed. This was more than unexpected, an oyster disclosing a pearl. The farther down Adi hiked—on occasion sliding his rump down scraggly rock faces—the greener and mistier it appeared, at one point triggering anxiety that he might be experiencing his first mirage. He stopped to guzzle one of his water bottles as an antidote to a sham oasis. Behind him the land heaved upward in a dingy mosaic of taupe and saffron and olive and rose; ahead of him it cleaved into a jungly channel lidded with silver fog.

This was what remained of the cloud forest, he realized entering it—the wet leafy cloak that'd once draped the entirety of Santa Flora. Thick squat trees shaped like spiders dripped cool water onto his scalp. Fern fronds brushed his pant legs. Moss-furred roots and vines wrestled underfoot and on every rock and stump was a marbling of lichens. A thousand stems in a thousand colors stretched toward the fog-drenched canopy where the leaves quivered from the weight of flitting birds. Adi wandered through this damp gnarled sanctuary as through a dream not his own—a dinosaur's dream, or an orchid's, or the deathbed memory of a shriveled island summoning its glistening green prime.

How and why the goats had spared this forested chute felt like an unworkable riddle until Adi came upon a window lake, a blue eyeball of fresh water lashed with spiked sedges and bowed waterlilies, and then another after that, linked by mucky seepage and skeins of shallow streams. The soused lushness of this pocket must've been sufficient to withstand the goats' predation, he figured; at the higher elevations, on the slopes and ridges, the trees themselves would've provided the water by trapping the fog. But tearing the trees apart, devouring them branch by branch, the goats had destroyed all that. He stood surveying the teeming green gloom, his face streaked not with sweat—beneath the canopy it was air-conditioner cool—but with rivulets of condensed fog. This was what the goats had spoiled, he thought. This was what they'd ripped from the island.

The forest petered out well before the eastern shore, where the valley opened to a wide rocky beach studded with sedge grasses where several dozen goats were grazing amid several more dozen fur seals. How Adi would contend with this interspecies mingling—he cringed at the prospect of witnesses to his slaughter, flippered or otherwise—was a problem for another day. By this time the sun was almost behind the mountains, a stripe of violet tingeing the eastern horizon. The going would be easier from here, he believed, but it wouldn't be quick. He followed the coastline north, weaving between clumps of basking seals that like the goats seemed indifferent to his presence; all he attracted were a few drowsily irritated snorts. When the sun sank and the island went dark he navigated by headlamp, imagining a satellite's view of a single minuscule light creeping northward in the midst of hundreds and hundreds of kilometers of black.

But Adi's wasn't the only light. Close to midnight, as he rounded the northeastern end, Adi came upon a wobbly yellow glow not far in the distance; this was so unexpected, like the cloud forest, that it took him a moment to recognize it as a fire. As he slunk closer he could see the firelight bouncing on the walls of what looked like a twin of his own sealers' hut, then a shadow moving fast across it. A man, he thought, with more bewilderment than alarm—it made no sense for the naval sailors to have returned—and for several minutes he stood motionless on the beach considering if and how he should approach.

He needn't have. A shaky white spotlight suddenly blinded him, bright as an eighteen-wheeler's headlight beam. Someone was moving fast toward him—no, two someones—while shouting at him and at the other and then at him again in hoarse, jumbled voices. Peering between his fingers, his left hand splayed against the light, Adi jerked at the sight of a pistol aimed squarely at his chest. *Drop the goddamn rifle,* they were yelling, *drop it now.*

What the two men wanted to know—the gunpoint question they kept shouting at him over and over again—was whether Adi was government. *No,* Adi kept saying, *no,* trying but plainly failing to parse the distinction between a government and a multinational nonprofit foundation. Only when he said, *I'm just here to shoot the goats,* did the shouting finally ebb.

The men stood frowning at each other and then back at Adi until the one without the gun broke into croaks of laughter. Then the gunman laughed too. *The goats?* he said, casting the spotlight briefly down to where Adi's rifle was lying beside him in the sand.

Adi said, *The foundation—they sent me here for five weeks. To—to eradicate the goats.*

Again the men traded glances before crumpling into deeper laughter; Adi was beginning to apprehend they were drunk. Owing to the glare of the spotlight he couldn't make out much else about them except that both were shirtless and the gunman's face and arms and even hands appeared covered in tattoos.

You're on Santa Flora, the gunman said slowly, *to kill goats.*

Shit, that's crazy, said the other, still laughing, wiping his eye.

Adi's headlamp beam flashed upon the gun muzzle, its cyclops eye just two meters from his sternum. His mouth felt so cobwebbed he wasn't sure he could speak. *That's—please, yes, that's right.*

That was you we saw, the gunman said, *that was you dragging a dead goat around the other day,* and with this Adi registered that these men must be the fishermen he'd spotted out at sea—presumably the nasty bastards the captain had warned him about.

That was me, he said. *Yes.*

Killing goats, the gunman said acidly, still shy of convinced. He swirled the pistol around as though to encompass the beach, the mountains, the island. *Here.*

That's what they hired me to do, Adi said.

Who did?

The foundation.

The other one asked, *They pay you for that?*

Adi nodded toward the voice.

How much?

The man greeted the amount with a low whistle. *Shit, that's crazy.*

Not bad for five weeks at a shooting gallery, the gunman said. The men clearly weren't from the capital, Adi thought; no one there would deem his salary worthy of a whistle. *Where's your camp?*

On the other end of the island.

Where's your boat? We didn't hear any boat.

I don't have a boat.

You crossed the island on foot?

Adi nodded.

Shit, that's crazy, the other man said.

The gunman asked again, *You're not government? You look like government. That's a government haircut.*

I'm just here to shoot the goats, Adi said. *That's my job. I swear.*

The gunman clicked off the spotlight, and as Adi's eyes adjusted, he could finally make out the man's face in the firelight: lean and slot-mouthed and almost entirely inked with smudgy-looking tattoos. The tattoos flowed down onto his shirtless chest, hollow and hairless, and sleeved a pair of rangy, veiny arms. Whatever government looked like, this was its opposite. He swished the pistol at Adi, grinning a gap-toothed grin. *Then welcome to Campo Langosta, I guess.*

Shittiest resort in the Pacific but the drinks are free. You might as well stay for some.

But, stalling, fumbling, wanting anything anywhere else in the world, *I . . .*

Come on, the gunman growled, turning and walking and beckoning with the pistol for Adi to follow. *Seems we're all in the slaughter together.*

The men claimed a pair of metal folding chairs set beside the campfire; Adi found a seat on a big knob of driftwood. Almost immediately the gunman went rummaging through a small tackle box beneath his chair while the other man passed an unlabeled liter of clear liquid to Adi.

Adi sniffed it and winced: cut-rate aguardiente, he guessed, not ruling out kerosene. Though he wanted none of it, his invitation to drinks had been at gunpoint. He took a pinched sip while stealing glances at the gunman, who after piercing a cigarette filter with a syringe needle was drawing something liquid from a shot glass. When the gunman was done he tossed the cigarette filter over his shoulder and set the syringe on his knee and wiggled his left arm like he was trying to shake the tattoos off it.

The gunman went by Grejo, Adi gathered after a while. Grejo called the other man Barrigón, other times Hulk. But mostly he called him Chuky.

Those are some candy shoes, Grejo said, jutting his chin toward Adi's feet while tying what looked to be a length of thick fishing leader around his bicep. Adi looked down at his hiking boots with their split-grain leather and polyurethane midsoles and skidded his feet back toward the driftwood, like one of his former fourth graders called out on a pair of outmoded sneakers. But the way Grejo was leering at them kindled a new fear: that the men could rob and kill him—for his rifle, his pack, his candy shoes—with hardly any jeopardy at all. Even if they left his body here by the campfire it wouldn't be discovered for more than a month, if ever. Caressing his elbow crook and still eyeing Adi's shoes Grejo said, *You must be from the capital.*

Adi turned away as the needle found its vein, scanning the other man for a reaction but finding none. Chuky's face was pockmarked and flat-browed with heavy, sagging eyelids that might've been extra-weighted by the liquor. He sat with his legs splayed wide to accommodate a big sunburned belly that bounced up and down when he laughed, which like hiccups was frequently and haphazardly.

Where are you from? Adi asked him.

He merely craned his neck sideways as if to say: *that way.*

It's a long way from anywhere to fish, Adi said, trying to make conversation but instantly regretting the potential suspicion in his tone. To patch it up he added, *The fishing must be good here.*

It's a long way from the capital to pop goats, said Grejo, despite the rebuke his voice already sounding mellower—syrupy even. He shrugged with one shoulder, still gently plunging the syringe contents into his arm. *You go where the fishes go.* Another shrug. *The fishes go here.*

What are you shooting? Chuky said, twirling a thick finger at Adi's rifle. *Is that a thirty-aught-six? Hand it over this way.*

Adi flinched but passed it to him. At the moment he wasn't worried about the man turning the rifle on him, though later it occurred to him how quickly his own murder could have been deemed a suicide. *The loneliness must've broken our poor Mister Killer,* the sailors would cluck over his body. *His son dying then his wife leaving him,* his former colleagues would say, shaking their heads. *The hurt was just too much for him.*

Chuky was inspecting the rifle, turning it in his hands not unlike the way Adi had examined the goat horn hours before. He aimed it over the fire and mimed a shot: *Bam!* Then he asked Adi, *How many goats do you kill in a day?*

Just a few so far. I've—I've just started.

A few? A grunt. *I could kill fifty from right here, sitting in my underwear. They should give me your job.*

Probably so, Adi said.

German optics, he said admiringly. *Bet you could see straight up a lizard's skirt with that scope.* Up and down went his belly. *Shit, that's crazy.*

He passed the rifle back to Adi followed by the liter of aguardiente. Even a dribble of it scalded Adi's throat, and he was unable to hide his grimace. Chuky noticed and chortled as he reclaimed the bottle. *Mother's milk,* he said, waggling his eyebrows. Then he pointed at Adi's forehead and asked, *What happened to your face?*

Adi's fingers jumped to the arc-shaped scab from where the rifle scope had kicked him, and to keep it hidden he stuck them there awhile. *Oh that,* he said. *I fell. I tripped on—some wet rocks.*

Bet they give you extra hazard pay for that, he said.

In the smoky near distance, by their hut, Adi could make out a dozen soot-colored triangles hanging on a line of rope, strung like drying laundry. For a moment he mistook them for flags until he saw another dozen spread atop a wooden pallet. He squinted then blenched. These were shark fins, he grasped, vaguely aware that the government had outlawed shark-finning years ago. Once or twice a year the newspapers ran stories about the cratering shark populations and the government's efforts to stem the illegal trade. *What are you fishing for?* he asked, opting to play dumb. *Tuna?*

Sure, said Grejo, flinging the spent syringe into the fire. He smiled. *Tuna.*

Tuna sharks, said Chuky, jellying himself with laughter.

We catch what people want to buy, Grejo said. *Not what the government tells us to catch. All you cocksuckers in the capital.*

Those are—they're fins, Adi said, raising a finger per his old wont, as though God would want to explain any of this.

Yeah, fins. The Chinese are crazy for shark fins. The government's crazy in the other direction.

Cocksuckers, Chuky mumbled, cradling the bottle atop his belly, nestling its spout in his shiny cleavage.

Grejo leaned forward and said, *Tell me something,* his voice beginning to ooze out of him now, as the effects of whatever he'd injected started to take hold, the roundness and stillness of his eyes reminding Adi of the gun muzzle that just fifteen minutes before had been glowering at his chest. *The people that hired you—what've they got against the goats?*

They're invasive, Adi said. *The goats aren't supposed to be here.*

Says who? The government?

Says nature.

Grejo sank scowling back into his chair as though stung by Adi's answer. *Says nature. I've been on the water since I was eight years old. And here's what I know.* He waved away smoke drifting into his face. *Nature don't give a fuck.*

Adi combined a nod with a shrug, the most neutral response he could muster.

No one even lives here, said Chuky, trying to light a cigarette but foiled by a laugh.

What I'm saying is, nature don't give *a fuck,* said Grejo, his tone different now, hotter, ignited by something. Maybe by whatever was floating through his bloodstream—Adi didn't know. Grejo snapped his fingers for the cigarettes to be passed and lit one but after a single long drag, Adi noticed, never smoked it again, instead clasping it between his fingers like a personal incense stick. He said, *It don't give a fuck.*

For what felt to Adi like an awfully long while they sat together in a flickering silence broken only by the fire's hiss and crackle and Chuky's random chortles, bubbling out of him like venting gases. Adi spent this time wondering how he might escape them: could he slip away tonight, if and when they passed out, or would that constitute some kind of mortal offense? And could he even make it back in the dark? The men were loose-brained now, dulled by aguardiente and whatever narcotic Grejo had shot into himself, but the morning sun might deliver a hard-nosed clarity, the kind that could get Adi killed. Whether or not he wanted to go on living was a question that'd been lashing him ever since his son died, but this felt separate from that; Adi was certain he didn't want to be murdered.

I'm thinking something funny, Grejo finally said, flinging the unsmoked cigarette into the fire and flashing Adi a dim, groggy smile.

Adi said, *What's that.*

They're paying you, what, doctor's wages to shoot up a bunch of goats with a thousand-dollar rifle, he said. Adi started to correct the doctor's wages but Grejo kept on: *While we're spending every goddamn minute looking over our shoulders for naval patrols. Spending half our profits paying them off. Spending the other half chugging all the way to goddamn Esmeraldas to avoid inspection and spending the third half we don't even have paying off the harbormaster there. Sleeping with this*—he yanked out the pistol from where it'd been tucked into the back of his shorts and brandished it beside his jaw—*every night on my goddamn pillow, like it's a girlfriend. Like it needs a kiss good night and a kiss good morning.*

Without removing his eyes from Adi he turned his head to kiss the barrel then slowly lowered it until it was pointed level with Adi's forehead. *For what, huh? For what? I'm asking you a question.*

I don't know.

Only now, studying Grejo's face for any signal that the trigger was about to be pulled, did Adi finally make out the tattoos overspreading it. They were sea creatures, all of them: a moray eel coiled across his forehead; an octopus on one cheek, a jellyfish on the other; a scallop shell on his chin; an open-mouthed tiger shark poised to clamp his jugular vein; a giant manta ray winged across his heart. Even his trigger finger was marked with the ocean: the leg of a starfish. Above the gun muzzle Adi watched Grejo's eyes twitch, watched his mouth compress into a thin hard line. The other man's expression might clue him into the threat of the situation, Adi thought, but he didn't dare glance away. Without blinking he watched Grejo's face and the muzzle trembling together in the firelight.

For sharks, he finally said, like the punchline to a

joke Adi didn't understand. With a snort he pointed his left finger at his neck, where the tiger shark swam. *For a few fucking sharks.*

All Adi could do was swallow while across Grejo's face spread the most vacant smile he'd ever seen. *That's funny, right?* Only when the gun dropped, eventually coming to rest atop Grejo's thigh, did Adi realize he hadn't been breathing; air leaked from his lungs as if from a slashed tire.

See, somebody in the government says we need more sharks, he went on. *And somebody else says we need fewer goats. More sharks. Less goats.*

The smile returned, broader and toothier this time, almost ghoulish in the firelight: *So they pay you for what you're doing and for what I'm doing they try to seize my boat and dump me in prison for twenty years. Even though it's the same thing. The same goddamn thing.*

He leaned forward to replace the gun back into his shorts, the whole time wagging his head. *So that's what's funny,* he said. *That's what.*

No one spoke until Chuky shuddered his head and this time without laughing said, *Shit, that's crazy.*

Adi chose to leave in the darkness. The man called Chuky fell unconscious first, the near-empty liter of aguardiente balanced impossibly on his chest, his laughing replaced with jagged snoring. Sometime later the one named Grejo decided to lie on his back to mull the constellations and within minutes let his eyelids draw shut.

Dawn broke before Adi had even reached the cloud forest. In the morning light an effervescence of seabirds circled and squawked and the mountains glowed pink as coral. Adi kept glancing back as he hiked, fearful that the shark finners might be in pursuit. When at last he made it back to Eremos Cove, where a hungry Santa Flora Reed Warbler and what appeared to be that same original phalanx of seven nanny goats were awaiting him, the sun was already tilting westward. He fed E3 and then, so physically sapped that even mere sentience felt too strenuous, fell onto his bed and didn't move until it was dark again.

What he saw, when he awoke, was a pair of eyes peering at him. Semiconscious, and still flooded with paranoia from the night before, Adi scrambled sideways off his bed to flee whomever or whatever was staring at him. But when at last he fumbled his headlamp on he saw that the eyes belonged to an animal: a smallish gray rat sitting on the sill of the crude opening beside his bed, twitching its nose in the halogen glow. *Jesus*, Adi said, relieved that it wasn't Grejo with his pistol or his laughing-gassed partner but less than pleased to be squaring off with a rat.

Still twitching its nose, the rat rose to its hind legs as though to beg food or maybe Adi's acquaintance, folding its hairless pink forepaws against its chest as though gripping an invisible cap. This was not how rats in the capital behaved. They slinked, they scurried, at the merest brush with humans they ducked under dumpsters or into storm drains. Adi tried shooing the rat by waving a hand at it but the rat stayed put. *Go away*, Adi snarled, but again, like the seven nanny goats that for all Adi knew were still parked outside his hut, it just blinked at him.

What was it, he asked himself, about the wildlife on Santa Flora? The goats, the seals, and now the rat: they'd all missed the headlines about mankind's threat. They seemed to size him up as an interloper at worst and at best, like the rat, as a harmless tourist, one potentially bearing gifts. They all behaved the way his son Jairo used to—fearless not from bravery but from an otherworldly strain of guilelessness, from a naivete untempered by instinct or awareness or in Jairo's case just the hard plain facts of earthly existence that his parents—his mother especially—had tried and tried to instill. Nature *did* give a fuck, they all seemed to believe. Why wouldn't it?

Get out! Adi shouted, this time hurling his pillow at the opening and this time convincing the rat that whatever welcome it thought was in the offing had been denied. The rat went scampering backward, whipping its long pink tail as it retreated into the darkness.

It must've smelled his food stores, Adi decided, skimming his flashlight over the pantry staples stacked in a corner with their uniform famine-relief logos. Fair enough, he supposed. Rats were rats and couldn't be otherwise. Adi would need to engineer a way to seal up the opening—a shame, because he'd become fond of the cool iodine breeze that flowed through it while he slept. How the rat or more likely its ancestors had arrived on Santa Flora didn't pose any great mystery: they'd probably disembarked from the same ships that'd seeded the goats here, castaways from London or Nantucket or from wherever whaling ships used to hail. They'd no doubt exacted their own toll on the island's native plants and birds and reptiles, furtive accessories to the goats' more conspicuous ravages. Laying waste to Santa Flora, he thought, must've been a collaborative effort. The goats just took all the blame.

With nothing to occupy him until sunrise, Adi eventually dug the horn from his backpack. It was a nice souvenir—the kind of thing he would've enjoyed bringing back for Jairo. But it needed a thorough cleaning, and so armed with a dish scrub and soap he headed to the cove under a starless black sky. Along the way he passed the seven nanny goats, who were bedded down in the sand in almost a circle, as though gathered for a faculty meeting or a canasta game. *Good evening, ladies,* he said aloud.

The absurdity struck him as he began washing the horn: that in the last twenty-four hours he'd had a gun pointed at him but they hadn't.

However many weeks it'd spent in the hot sun had left the horn mostly clean. All that was needed was for Adi to scrape away some bits of jerked flesh and death gristle from the base and scrub it inside and out. Sloshing soapy salt water back and forth, he found himself wishing for a pipe cleaner or swab to scour the interior the way he used to clean his clarinets. And that's what sparked the idea.

He got his first clarinet, a sticky-keyed rental, at eleven—the same age as Jairo on his death certificate. Adi hated it at first: the haphazard-seeming way its keys were arrayed; the feeble buzz that accompanied his low notes and the squeaks that popped like sonic pimples when he'd reach for a high note; and the total absence of clarinets from any of the music he heard on the radio. Even the look of it dismayed him. While the popular girls were elegantly bowing their violins and cellos, and the beefy boys were plucking their double basses without the slightest hint of effort, Adi sat struggling with an oversized licorice stick.

Then his grandfather learned he'd started playing it. One afternoon he ushered Adi into his study—a cluttery, smoke-stained room the grandchildren were forbidden to enter—and pulled a dozen record albums from his shelves: American jazz from the early twentieth century, most of it from New Orleans. One of his grandfather's ears had been deafened by shrapnel during the revolution, so everything he did—listening to music especially—was done at a tilt. Yet Adi found himself likewise tilting, as though his ears were being pulled, when his grandfather dropped the needle onto the first song, Israel Gorman on "When the Swallows Come Back to Capistrano": a clarinet could do more than honk and squeak, Adi realized, it could scream and whisper and laugh and weep and slither and growl and stammer and wail. It could *say* things—things that couldn't otherwise be said. But when his grandfather played Albert Burbank's "Burgundy Street Blues," with its birdlike trills and weird bluesy warbles, Adi felt as though the chair and every other object in the room—maybe in the world—had suddenly and irrevocably fallen away.

Adi didn't know what exactly he could do with the dripping goat horn in his hands, but he was dimly aware that maybe Vikings—or maybe it was early Hebrews, or both—had once made music with goat horns. The nanny goats watched as Adi hurried back to his hut, where from the foundation's toolbox he gathered the saw and the drill and a handful of bits.

With some minor difficulty he sawed the narrow tip from the horn, surprised to find it solid even several centimeters from the end. He was about to saw farther down but, reconsidering, instead drilled a hole through the freshly blunted end. He found he could blow through the horn after that, though minus much of any sound. Enlarging the mouth hole with a thicker bit, however, yielded Adi what he was seeking: a raspy, fluctuant, primitive-sounding note—an A-flat, if he wasn't mistaken. By drilling holes into the side, four for his fingertips and one, on the opposite side, for his thumb, Adi was able to finger a discordant scale. He kept at it, humming mindlessly in the dark the way the captain had, expanding and re-expanding the finger holes with larger and larger bits, his fingers caked with keratin dust.

When Deyanira was pregnant with Jairo, Adi used to play his clarinet to her swollen belly, wanting his child even in utero to experience the same revelatory sensations he'd felt in his grandfather's study and that his wife—he believed back then, and maybe still did—had experienced the first time she ever saw Adi, playing Albert Burbank solos in a basement jazz club in the capital.

He'd been surprised to see her in the audience that night. Adi's band, with his best friend Matias on the drums, tended to draw elderly sophisticates, old men in linen suits sipping Havana Club and passing notes to the stage with requests for sentimental obscurities. Lissome and dark-eyed, Deyanira was alongside one of those old men, a devoted regular with slicked-back silver hair and a reputation as a minor crime boss. He'd always been delighted with Adi's repertoire and solos but was the opposite of delighted to see his granddaughter sitting across from Adi during a stage break, twirling a strand of black hair in the candlelight, squandering her future. He'd never approved of her marriage to a basement clarinetist turned schoolteacher; in retrospect, Adi supposed, neither had she.

Dawn was breaking as Adi finished tuning the goat horn, a soft pink light blushing the open hut door. The horn's register was limited—a minor diatonic scale—but Adi found that by dampening the end with two fingers, not unlike the way a French horn player plunges the bell, he could bend the notes down a half step, expanding his palette. Its tones were husky and ancient sounding—primordial, really—but Adi didn't dislike it; an approximation of an Albert Nicholas riff, from "Clarinet Blues," sounded both familiar and alien, Storyville filtered through the Stone Age, the lonesome goatherd blues.

E_3 seemed fond of it, anyway. The little bird was startled by the horn at first, making a fluttery retreat to the Ninja Turtle's side, but after a while the bird peered up almost curiously as Adi kept playing for it, cocking its head at the blue notes and at one point— Adi knew this wasn't the case but allowed himself some mild enchantment—appearing to shuffle its feet in raggedy time to the music. *That's called jazz,* he said to the bird. *The mating songs of my species.*

If he'd smiled on Santa Flora before this moment, Adi couldn't recall it. He only registered that he was smiling, in fact, because the sensation felt so foreign to him, akin to his grandfather regaining hearing in his shrapnel-blasted ear, Jelly Roll Morton suddenly flowering in full stereo. Twice yesterday Adi had stared down a gun barrel, aimed first at his chest and then at his head; he wondered if perhaps the smile was a delayed reaction to that, relief displacing terror at last, his body—if not his mind, not entirely—exulting at the sight of another sunrise, at his own extinction averted.

But after a moment Adi recognized the odd smile as a kind of physical echo: eleven years before he'd stood over Jairo's crib playing these same songs to his infant son on his clarinet, watching Jairo's fat bronze legs kicking and a look of tickled fascination beshining his face. Immediately Adi steeled himself for the psychic plunge that tended to trail such remembrances, for the now-routine heart sink that'd just a month ago hollowed him out in a barber's chair, the same barbershop where he and Jairo used to get their hair cut together falling abruptly silent, not a single pair of scissors clacking as every barber and every customer turned their eyes to the man rocking slowly back and forth in the chair with his head in his hands, ten men squirming as they watched Adi crumple.

But the crumpling didn't come, not this time, and Adi chose not to ask why. *Here's one,* he said to the bird, *you'll like this,* blowing for it a deeply paraphrased version of "Stella by Starlight," one of Jairo's regular lullabies.

But then from outside, midway through, intruded another sound, and lowering his horn Adi realized that one of the nanny goats was bleating softly, almost cooing. He stepped to the open door. A charcoal-splotched goat with a black bandit mask was standing apart from the others, training her bleats toward the hut. She looked, to Adi, oddly wistful, as though the melody had been familiar to her. *She's almost in key,* he said to the bird. *We'll call her Harmony.*

Turning back, Adi noticed that the rat had returned. It was up on its hind legs in the opening with its pink forepaws folded in front of it, as before—though more meekly this time, as if hoping to apologize for its earlier trespass, or perhaps to compliment the music. Whatever their ecological crimes, Adi thought, Santa Flora's rats had exemplary manners.

Fine then, Adi grumbled, *fine,* fetching and unwrapping one of the E3 bars from his stockpile—he and the bird certainly weren't going to eat them all—and setting it opposite the rat on the sill. The rat went scooting over to it as soon as Adi released it, a half second of sniffing preceding a half hour of gnawing. Again Adi found himself smiling. Whether this smile was an echo or not, he couldn't tell. It seemed possible that all he had left were echoes, an interior album of only cover songs. But he couldn't help savoring the feel of it anyway. As the remnant of cloud forest was to Santa Flora, it felt like proof that some part of him, however small, was somehow still alive.

After a while Adi returned the goat horn to his lips and blew a gentle if mangled rendition of Acker Bilk's "Stranger on the Shore," watching E3 bobbing its shaggy-feathered head and the rat he decided to call Oliver for Oliver Twist eating the famine-relief bar down to a contented crumb-less nothingness that, for a few shimmery moments at least, mirrored Adi's mind.

Sunday morning on Santa Flora, that tiny dislocated comma out in the horse latitudes. Stirless, sun-doused. The sea so calm as to suggest it'd decided to sleep in, its waves brushing up like the untroubled breaths of a slumbering giant. Even on the island's windward side, where Eremos Cove was nestled, the palm fronds hung motionless, their regular shoosh gone silent. The sky too was idle, exerting only a few cirrus vapors, half-hearted white brushstrokes on an otherwise blank blue canvas. Likewise the island's goats, who lazed in groups up and down the slopes with their forelegs tucked beneath their chests, drowsily surveying the lithoid stillness.

Sundays, when Adi was a child, meant visiting his grandparents, the routine so fixed it verged on ritual: his parents trading newspaper sections on the crosstown bus ride while his big sister, Ana, read teen romance novels and Adi drew fingertip doodles on the window grime; his Wela worrying her giant pot of sancocho on the stovetop, testing and retesting it with her wooden spoon and lamenting, never quite sincerely, that it wouldn't live up to last week's glories; his older cousins sprawled in front of the television or out back smoking cigarettes filched from the open packs their grandfather left everywhere; and Abuelo himself leading Adi into his study to hear his latest clarinet piece, the old man tipping his good ear toward the clarinet bell with his eyes shut and with a beatific, dreamlike expression on his face, the same expression the mortician—surely by chance—somehow managed to sculpt onto his face for the casket viewing.

Sundays with Jairo had been even more fixed—though by Jairo's direction, not Adi's. What the doctors called *cognitive rigidity* was a cornerstone of Jairo's neurological condition, diagnosed at eighteen months when struggles with walking and speaking appeared. *Neurodivergent* had been their term. *Special,* Deyanira's. Sundays, by the time Jairo was six, were for paper airplanes: one hundred of them—no more, no less—designed and folded in the morning and flown in the afternoon, usually from the top bleachers at the high school football stadium down into the empty parking lot. On Jairo's face, always, was that same look of tickled curiosity that Adi had glimpsed over the end of his clarinet when playing for him in his crib: something less than a smile, because Jairo was always stingy with those, but exponentially more than the thought-clogged frown he wore throughout most days. It might've been owing to basic genetics, but Jairo's expression often reminded Adi of his grandfather's: dreamy, sated, slightly listing. At times Adi would see it lingering on Jairo's face even after the planes had finished coasting, when down on the asphalt Adi would be collecting a hundred white triangles into a paper shopping bag and, peering upward, catch sight of his son, ten meters up on the top bleacher, seemingly aware of nothing save the sky, stoned with the beauty of flight whose sublimity only he could fully measure.

On Santa Flora, however, all that needed collecting was driftwood for the evening's fire. The foundation would surely want him out shooting today—there'd been no discussions about weekends or days off, and as the gunman's partner had suggested, Adi's kill count remained meager. But then the foundation hadn't mentioned that what Santa Flora lacked in horizontal size it made up for in grueling verticality, or, more critically, had failed to warn him that he might find himself staring down a gun barrel not once but twice. A sabbath respite felt justified. Dozy and languid, the island itself seemed to endorse it.

The seven nanny goats watched as over and over again Adi walked barefooted to the cove and came back carrying dry tentacles of driftwood, which he piled not far from them on the sand. He was beginning to tell them apart now: not just Harmony, the singer, but the other six. Their horns varied, for starters: some blunt, some long, one pair curled at the ends and another pair twisted like helices. Five of them had thick wavy coats; two had short hair, as though fresh from the salon. One with big procumbent teeth Adi started calling Booska, after a cartoon character Jairo had been fond of. Another pawed constantly in the sand, as though futilely searching for something, and Adi called this one Contact Lens. Still another displayed the alarming ability to rotate her head nearly 180 degrees in order to rake her hind legs. This one Adi named Linda Blair.

Two of the goats, Booska and Harmony, trailed Adi to the cove when, after gathering the driftwood, he stripped to his underwear for a swim. In the last couple of days he'd noticed several of them licking the stones or leaves where he'd urinated, presumably craving some mineral he was excreting. Their signal now, he figured, must've been seeing him in his underwear, since that's what he was always wearing when he'd come rolling out of the hut for his morning pee. But soon he found himself wondering: If they were smart enough to deduce this, what might they have divined about him stepping out of the hut with the rifle slung over his shoulder, about his target practice on the other side of the hut, about the gunshots echoing over the ridge, about the charred goat bones still scattered in the firepit?

If the pair had in any way contemplated these things or, more immediately, were disappointed he wasn't peeing, they didn't show it. Instead, by the water's edge, the goats plopped themselves in the sand and watched Adi wade into the glassy cove until, with a quick dive, he disappeared beneath it. For as long as his lungs allowed he stayed submerged, fanning his arms and legs in the warm blue womb that'd borne Santa Flora and all its native life, for that single extended breath feeling profoundly alone yet also, queerly, somehow not alone, as though in that teeming silence his cells were dimly recalling some ancient consonance.

The first thing Adi saw, when he surfaced, were the two goats surveilling him with nonchalant lifeguard stares: alone, again, yet not alone. When Adi paddled to the left, the goats' gaze followed; same to the right. He resisted gleaning comfort from this. Tomorrow, he knew, he would have to resume killing their brothers, their fathers, their sons, their uncles, their nephews. Yet for an ineluctable moment he felt himself buoyed by a lightness so peculiar it verged on the absurd: a man marooned on a desert island—with only an extinct bird and a mannerly rat and seven doomed goats for company—somehow feeling, after all those desolate months, not quite lonesome.

The way people avoid you after the death of a child was something Adi hadn't anticipated. Fellow parents from school making U-turns in the grocery aisle to dodge him, or piloting their strollers off the park path when they'd spot him jogging. Colleagues hurrying out of meetings to elude small talk. Never from malice, he'd understood, but instead from fear: everyone afraid he'd talk about it and equally afraid he wouldn't. Even with those who didn't or couldn't avoid him, the awkwardness felt pressurized: the way some acquaintances sidestepped talking about their own children, as though fearing that doing so would be akin to gloating, or worse, the one or two who took to complaining about their kids—the mess, the chaos, the byzantine winter football league schedule—as if to imply some grotesque silver lining, that your life might be gutted but at least you're not stepping on Legos in the dark.

And then Deyanira, who'd blamed Adi. Who'd

tried putting a gun in his hands as though sloppy retribution could somehow undo it. Who'd packed her life into four rolling suitcases because he refused. But Adi couldn't think about that now or maybe ever.

Back inside the hut he brushed the last remaining flecks of goat meat off his palm into E3's box. *That's the end of it*, he announced to the bird, adding: *uh-oh*. Since killing that first goat, Adi had been sun-drying the few leftover scraps of it in various locales: first on a slab of basalt at the edge of the cove, until the crabs swarmed it; then atop his hut roof, until something else found it (most likely Oliver, it occurred to him now); and finally tied with string and hung from buttonwood branches where various seabirds, lizards, and a nightmarishly large black centipede—longer than Adi's foot—kept paring it down. The constant pilfering, though, was only part of the problem. The drier the meat had gotten, the less fond of it E3 seemed. Sometimes the bird dashed the tiny bits around the box with its beak, as if to rouse them and maybe rehydrate them.

Let's try this, Adi said, opening a can of mackerel and flaking bits of it into the box. The bird hopped over to examine them but very clearly recoiled at the scent. Its withering frown mirrored that of the old woman in the wall portrait. *Really can't blame you*, said

Adi. *Not my favorite either. But you have to eat. Otherwise you actually will go extinct.* Adi and Deyanira's tactic, when Jairo had refused certain foods, was to leave him alone with his plate in the kitchen for a while; often, when they'd return, the food would have vanished. It was difficult to be picky, went their thinking, when you had nothing else to pick from. *Maybe pretend you're a seagull,* Adi said to E3, the unamused bird looping its gaze from Adi to the mackerel then back again. All Adi could do for now was hope that, like Jairo, E3 would eventually make peace with its lunch. He left the T-shirt off the top of the box so that every now and then he could monitor the bird's progress.

For Oliver, he set an E3 bar on the sill. And thereupon arrived another idea: an experiment of sorts, more impetuous than considered. He unwrapped another E3 bar and carried it outside to where the nanny goats were lounging, Harmony and Booska back among them.

Harmony was the first to rise as Adi approached. She was the doyenne of the group, he'd already determined; the others seemed to always be clearing the path for her, deferring to her headship, and while he'd witnessed her butting a few of them he'd never seen one butt her back. Dangling the E3 bar before him,

Adi watched her tensing as he crept forward. With each small step he took, the other goats began rising one by one to their hooves until they stood facing him like some expressionless jury or an eighth-grade class encountering a substitute teacher. *It's okay,* Adi tried assuring them. *It's not a trick.*

With a flare of her nostrils, Harmony lifted a front leg then stomped it back into the sand. Adi wasn't sure what this might mean: she could've been warning him to keep his distance but could as easily have been warning the other goats to stay back from her food. Yet none of the goats, so far as he could tell, were eyeballing the E3 bar; their stares were wholly fastened upon him. *It's delicious,* he told them, with a shake of the E3 bar, not quite registering the lie. Only a rat and a thousand orange crabs would corroborate that.

It didn't escape Adi that he was very nearly reenacting his first encounter with these same goats, when also in his underwear he'd advanced on them with the rifle. But that was then. This time he was offering food, a candy bar–shaped oblation, and maybe, in his mind anyway, some kind of fractional détente, an intra-island accord between exiled mammals whose blood, as he'd learned on his first nighttime slog, tasted exactly the same. He wanted them to know he'd been sent here to slaughter them but he wasn't going through with it. Not exactly, anyway. Not with them at least.

Harmony narrowed her eyes and sniffed the air. *That's right,* Adi whispered, inching closer. *It's different this time.*

But it wasn't. The sudden sneeze Harmony made was clearly an alarm, and a command to the others: every goat including her leapt sideways all at once, as if the force of the sneeze had blown them apart, and took off running in seven different directions. Adi stood there for a while with his arm still dumbly outstretched. He couldn't blame them, he supposed, listening to them bleating in the mangroves, finding one another in that green mire. He recalled his interviewer likening the goats to a cancer on Santa Flora. But wasn't he, to them, the same?

The seven goats didn't return until just before dark, when Adi was sitting beside the fire absently blowing his horn. They didn't come back warily or defiantly or in any way out of the ordinary. From a rustling of low palms appeared Harmony, with her black bandit mask, followed by Booska and Contact Lens and Linda Blair and the three others, and with barely a glance in Adi's direction they reclaimed their usual spot about twenty meters from the fire.

The first time Adi played "Stella by Starlight," cycling through his old club and crib-side standards, Harmony kept silent. But an hour later, when he played it again under a sky so star-spattered and cosmos-smeared that the song seemed not just befitting but ordained—this time Harmony joined in, rising to her hooves and bleating so gently and forlornly that after a while Adi lowered the horn to just listen. Her voice was deep and warbly, devoid of the staccato blats heard commonly up and down the island, and all the other goats yielded to her voice, choosing to listen like Adi was. Splitting his gaze between the starlight and the firelight, the only conclusion he could muster was that everything in nature, which meant everything everywhere, was more intricate and indecipherable than an outcast man on an obscure island could possibly fathom. The thought was a surrender yet in its wake trailed a peculiar solace, a sudden disburdening: if the questions couldn't be answered then the strain of asking them must be futile. After a while he laid himself down in a soft hollow of sand, still listening to her sing as his eyelids slipped closed.

In the stark morning sunlight two things became clear: E3 needed fresh meat to survive, and Adi, despite all the uncertainties and qualms perforating him, needed to resume his mission. The futile questioning needed to be over; now was time for the doing. As an aid or a spur, not unlike the motivational recordings his friend Matias was always plugging into his ears, Adi began playing his memory of his interviewer's voice on a near-constant loop: *The job is saving one of the Pacific Ocean's most unique and vibrant ecosystems from very certain destruction*, she'd said. *The job is preventing the assured extinction of at least eight more species of birds and five more species of reptiles and an entirely unknown number of plants . . .*

His route for the day, he decided, would be the same he'd taken to Campo Langosta—but the lower section only, south of the cloud forest. Whether he'd ever venture north of the cloud forest again, where the shark finners were, was the one question still worth weighing. The wisest move, it seemed to him, was to cede that half of the island to them for the time being; he didn't think he could withstand another staring contest with Grejo's gun barrel.

But this issue could wait until he'd eradicated all the billy goats from the southern half. Work the island in quadrants, they'd said. Clear the goats from one, then move to the next. Over his shoulder and across his chest he draped the nylon bandolier with its eighty slotted bullets. This time, he understood, he'd need to use them. *That's the job,* he heard her saying. *That's what it is.*

It was flatly impossible, of course, but word seemed to have spread among the billy goats to steer clear of him. After mucking his way through the mangroves and ascending the first ridge, he kept passing group after group of nanny goats—but not a single gang of billies. It was like strolling the streets of the capital when the Copa América football tournament was on TV: women and children only. It wasn't that he didn't see *any* billy goats: he spotted what he thought were a few, here and there embedded with the nannies, though unless he saw them urinating or happened to spy hanging testicles he couldn't always be sure; plus a couple of suspected bachelors that he decided were out of range; and, once, a young billy that peered over an outcrop at him in such a comically slapstick way, with popped eyes and a spluttery bleat of surprise, that gunfire didn't seem the fitting response.

Except that it was, technically.

Yet these weren't distinctions he'd been hired to sort, he told himself, threading his way through jagged heaps of streaky volcanic rubble and melancholy-looking bushes shorn of their leaves. *The job,* he heard her saying, *is removing a malignant growth that's been steadily erasing some of the most vulnerable and least studied flora and fauna on the bloody planet.* He knew he was being too finicky and dithery about shooting. *I could kill fifty from right here, sitting in my underwear,* Chuky had said. Was it possible, Adi wondered, that he was simply *wired* wrong for this? Or was killing something you could learn, like playing the clarinet?

Maybe what he needed to do was to channel E3, he thought: broken-winged; hungry; its very species all but extinct by the goats. If Adi couldn't pull the trigger, E3 would do it. But this line of imagining got him only so far. As he neared the eastern shoreline, with the seabirds starting to funnel overhead, squawking and skreeking in voices that for all he could tell were angry or alarmed or chatty and content, he felt himself pulled short by the disconnect. He couldn't think or feel like a bird. He could only think like a man.

But a different man, maybe: one less deliberative, less delicate, less honeycombed by questions and doubts. The man the captain had assumed him to be: the one he'd called Mister Killer. As Adi ascended the final ridge before the island went slanting into the sea he tried viewing the landscape through Mister Killer's eyes, noting not the pink-copper of the corrugated slopes, gilded by the late-morning sunlight, nor the infinitude of ocean behind him, drenching his pupils with its billion variants of blue, but scanning instead for signs of goat activity: for fresh scat, for movement, for the walnut-colored curve of horns amid the scrub. He tried ignoring the music of the breeze swishing the rusty bushes and the oscillating babel of the seabirds above to listen instead for the deep basso blats of billy goats, for the scritch of hooves troubling gravel. After a while he found himself even walking differently: more slowly, more steadily, more strategically. Like a predator. Like Mister Killer. Like the man the foundation thought they'd hired. And maybe Deyanira thought she'd married.

Then he saw it, as he came upon the leeward shore

and looked down, and as instantly as if he'd been shot he dropped to the ground: the shark finners' boat, sitting just outside the perimeter of a cove so intensely indigo that its waters must've plumbed near to the earth's core. He rolled behind a screen of thigh-high obsidian slabs and fumbled out his binoculars, winded already from the thunking of his heart. He edged the binoculars over a rock.

Adi was still clumsy about gauging distance, so he couldn't say how far from shore the boat was: too far to swim, he guessed, though just barely. He bellycrawled to his left toward an opening between the black slabs that offered a wider, more covert view.

The island didn't slant into the sea here, as it did farther north along the leeward coastline. Here it dropped abruptly down into an amphitheater of cliffs scored vertically with what looked like toothmarks, as though a massive chunk of the shore had been bitten off by a sea creature too immense to even imagine. How many meters down they dropped Adi was again unable to judge. Six stories at least. The same as his old apartment building.

Despite his shaky fingers he was able to focus the binoculars. There was Grejo, he saw, shirtless as before but with a purple bandanna atop his head and gray gloves on his hands, and beside him was Chuky, dressed in a red T-shirt and yellow shorts like some dissolute Winnie-the-Pooh.

They were positioned at the stern of the boat, where a metal ramp sloped into the water. Chuky appeared to be operating some sort of winch: Adi could see a thick black line slithering across the ramp as it went coiling onto a spool behind the cabin. Every so often the men paused the winch to unclip hooks from the line, tossing them into a pile near the cabin before resuming spooling the line.

Until a shark came dragging aboard. It looked big to Adi, as long as the men were tall, and he could see an inky black tip on its dorsal fin. As Chuky grabbed some kind of metal javelin or spear, the shark lay there on its belly with its upper half on the deck and lower half on the ramp. It must be dead, Adi thought, as still as it was. He'd never been fishing before; maybe sometimes the hooks killed the fish while other times they didn't. He didn't know.

Grejo moved a few steps back as Chuky raised the spear over his head and, with a violent grunt that Adi couldn't possibly have heard but swore he did, plunged it deep into the shark's back, just ahead of its dorsal fin. Then he stood there, feet planted wide, as the impaled shark—very definitely and very terribly alive—thrashed for what must've been a full minute. It whipped its tail and whipped its head and it whipped its tail and whipped its head as Chuky held it pinned to the deck and said something to Grejo that made him throw back his head in laughter.

Using the spear as a lever, Chuky heaved the shark deeper onto the deck while Adi saw Grejo pull a long knife from his belt, the blade flashing in the sunlight. Adi watched him crouch down to slice off the dorsal fin first, leaving a bright red ellipse on the shark's back; he watched an eruption of blood come streaming down its silver flanks. With the severed fin in one hand, Grejo crabwalked away to let the shark thrash some more, its tail and head flopping left and then right and its mouth gaping open as though to champ his captor's ankle or moan for mercy. When the thrashing ebbed, Grejo moved down to slice off the shark's tail fins, tossing them onto the deck where, Adi noted for the first time, dozens of others were strewn, the black-tipped and freshly red-rimmed dorsal fin at the top. The shark thrashed again, but more weakly this time.

Jesus, Adi whispered.

Now Grejo moved to the shark's head to yank the hook from its open mouth, and then, after a signal, Chuky wrenched the spear upward and out of the shark, its bottom stained red like it'd been dipped in paint. Chuky flipped the spear over and with the clean blunt end poked and pushed the shark until it was angled near the edge of the ramp. Then both men began kicking it in its blood-rilled side and its pale belly—one, two, four, six times—until at last the shark tipped off the ramp and back into the sea.

This time it was Grejo's turn to make his partner laugh. Adi could see the laughter roiling his red-shirted belly as he leaned the spear against the gunwale and shook a cigarette from a pack and lit it.

The binoculars slipped from Adi's eyes. He didn't know what he'd imagined the men did—hadn't even really considered it—but it wasn't this, could've never been this. Nausea that felt different from stomach nausea began to swamp him: more diffuse than stomach nausea, emanating from a place in his body he couldn't identify or point to, like maybe whatever and wherever the soul or conscience might be. Still shielded behind the slabs of obsidian he curled himself into a ball on the ground and clamped his eyelids closed to wait out the sickness.

But even with his eyes squeezed shut he could see the shark. It was slowly sinking into that indigo hole, nose first, unable to swim without its fins, dropping straight down like a boat anchor and trailing three plumes of blood that whirled crimson in Adi's mind even as the depths of the cove turned sapphire then purple then black. He felt the shark hit bottom, watched a cloud of sand envelop it, and then, when the sand veil settled, looked into its open eye. The shark was still alive, Adi knew, even at the earth's lightless floor. A minute passed. Then two. Adi tried opening his eyes but failed. The shark's eye was still open. The shark was still alive.

Only when he felt gut certain the shark was dead did Adi find the strength to wipe away the gravel pasted to his cheek and pull himself off the ground. With his legs outspread he sat with his back to the smooth rock, waiting for the last of the nausea to subside. What else didn't he know about how the world worked? The supermarket pork that week after week had swum in his Wela's sancocho: that he'd never considered the pigs that'd provided it was now a given. But he'd also never thought about the men who'd slaughtered them or the way they'd done so, whether they'd kicked the pigs as they lay bleeding and cracked jokes and lit cigarettes then scrubbed their hands and took the bus home and hugged their children as Porky Pig stuttered on the television screen. It'd always just been mute pink chunks under cellophane, like the shark fins heaped upon the deck.

With what he thought was great stealth, Adi pressed himself to the ground and trained his binoculars back onto the boat. The men were still suckling their cigarettes, their apparent reward for finning the shark. Grejo appeared to be telling some kind of joke or story, thrusting his hips back and forth, humping the air—Adi could guess what kind of story—that kept making Chuky jiggle and bend. *Shit, that's crazy*, Adi could almost hear him saying, as he turned from Grejo to wipe excess merriment from his eye.

Then Chuky pointed up at the cliff, suddenly—pointed directly to where Adi was—and Grejo leaned forward, squinting up to where Chuky was pointing with one hand shading his forehead—and waved.

Grejo was waving, and Grejo was grinning. Like a friend down the sidewalk, like a footballer to his fans, Grejo was standing there waving to Adi.

He dropped the binoculars and ducked back behind the rocks. The glare of the binocular glass reflecting the sunlight, he thought—they must've seen the bright flicker of it, *dammit*, just as Adi had seen the sunlight briefly torching Grejo's knife. Must've easily deduced who was watching them, because it could only have been Adi. And then—then *waved*.

Another subset of nausea squirmed him, the source of this one even harder to locate. Why would he possibly *wave*? They weren't in this together, Adi and them. They ought to have been aiming the pistol at him instead—firing off a couple of shots, even, to rid themselves of the threat they'd been too doped and drunk to neutralize back in the firelight. They were criminals and he was a witness; he needn't have married the granddaughter of a crime boss to know you always contained witnesses. In some absurd way he found himself *wishing* they'd shot at him instead: to cement their enmity, to stake the line between them. His job was to save the world—it'd said so right there in the job listing—while theirs was to maul it, to pilfer it, to strip it bare. A chill shivered him and bile rose inside his throat. When he belly-crawled away from the cliff edge, and finally rose to his feet behind the cover of a tall saltbush tree, he found himself staggering as though high on whatever narcotic sap ran through Grejo's veins. And in that way, throat-clogged, wobble-legged, canting left and right, he fled.

The dim goat paths were almost impossible to detect when hurrying. He traversed the first downward slope to the south, snaking his way between patinated rocks and scattered groves of more saltbush and buttonwood, and then, in that rough up and down of Santa Flora, ascended a loose scree-slope to the north. Far overhead, a gust of seabirds swooped and turned. It was hot and windless and with every fourth or fifth step the rocks made half-hearted attempts at an avalanche, dragging Adi backward.

Breathing hard, his ankles quavering, he was about to begin his descent at the crest of the second ridgeline when he came skidding to a rubbly stop. There before him, blocking his path, was the largest billy goat he'd yet to see on the island.

There was no mistaking this one. Its horns must've been as long as Adi's arms, with the same flying raptor silhouette as the other billy he'd killed. Its back half was shagged in cream-colored hair, thick and lucent in the sunlight, while the long hair on its neck and head was the color of coffee. It looked clean, unlike the other billy; brushed and groomed even, with a noble sheen to its unmatted coat. Its handsomeness, its size, its sturdy stance, made it appear to be posing for an official portrait: it exuded a measure of power and authority that brought to Adi's mind, queerly, his grandfather. If the billy had noticed Adi's approach, it didn't show it. It was staring downslope, away from him, as though immersed in some patriarchal vigil, a governor taking in the breadth of his province.

The rifle strap slipped from his shoulder if not precisely from instinct then from something just as automatic, as involuntary. *The job is saving one of the Pacific Ocean's most unique and vibrant ecosystems from very certain destruction,* he heard her saying. He flicked off the safety and angled his feet and slowly raised the barrel. *That's the job,* she was saying. *That's what it is.* But inside the scope, as if peering into a kaleidoscope, Adi saw not the billy goat in the crosshairs but rather the shark's open eye, drifting down through the blueness; saw the cloud forest as a pulsing green molecule laced with vines and dripping leaves; saw Harmony singing her dirges in the yellow glow of the firelight; saw the shark's blood pouring across its gills, wet red eclipsing wet silver; but superimposed over everything saw Grejo waving, saw the purple starfish on his hand swishing blithely, pledging Adi into the fraternity of killers. *It's the same goddamn thing,* he could hear him saying, the voice oozy and low-pitched and somehow incorporeal, a ghost keening from across the plane. The barrel swayed. It wasn't the same. It wasn't at all. Adi's finger nicked the trigger.

The billy goat's back legs buckled, for just a moment, as though he'd begun to kneel down, and then with a sharp pitchy cry he lurched forward into the brush and was gone.

Adi scuttled downslope to where he'd hit it, or maybe hit it—he wasn't sure. He scanned the ground for any signs of blood or hair and found none. He'd missed him, he thought. The billy had jumped and yawped from surprise not pain. Relief washed through him, but with it came a brick-hard certainty: he couldn't do this any longer. This might've been the only way to save Santa Flora but he couldn't be the one to save it.

Then came a cry—from due south, along the ridgeline, almost the same cry the billy goat had issued after the rifle crack. Adi ran toward it then stopped. A spot of fresh blood the size of his thumbnail dotted the round pate of a rock, and instantly Adi's relief curdled into shame. He'd wounded him. He'd been watching Grejo waving at him from inside the scope and by swaying the rifle barrel had shot him in the rear leg instead of the chest. *Oh God,* he whispered, repeating it frantically. As if in response, the billy goat issued another cry, this one more distant than the last: muffled even, as though he was howling underwater, leadenly sinking in a billowing red cloud. Adi moved toward it. It seemed obvious but no one had prepared him for this: that wayward shots could spell worse outcomes than true ones. The billy was suffering, Adi understood, and his only job now was to finish him.

As he stalked the ridgeline the blood trail intensified: a fleck on a leaf here, a drizzle on some rocks there. Inside a small cavity just beneath the ridge crest, a cool shadowed alcove, he found a pool of blood where the billy goat must've stopped to rest, the blood already turning rust-colored as the earth soaked it up. He kept on, twice losing the trail and needing to backtrack to find it. A tiny daub of crimson in a crevice; a smear on a fern frond that'd been chewed to a frazzle; spatters on a bed of low white flowers; another browning pool where the billy goat had tried resting. And every now and again, in the widening distance, that rending cry.

The billy goat kept heading downward—probably to take the weight off his rear leg, Adi figured. He passed a group of eight or nine nanny goats that were tearing into a bush, expecting harsh glowers from them but receiving only the same dull stares he always got, as though they'd failed to make the connection between the billy that'd gone by dripping blood and the frenzied man following it. The foundation, he realized, would've had him stop to mow them all down. *That's what it is,* he heard her saying.

Adi rolled his gaze over and across the ground ahead of him, scrambling from one droplet to the next not unlike the way Jairo used to hunt Easter eggs in the park. He followed the droplets into a dank gorge where violet shadows stained the rock walls and went splashing through a shallow pool of puce water where a spring fed the gorge. On the other side of the pool the blood trail disappeared; twenty minutes or more passed until he was able to locate it again. The gorge was so naturally dark that Adi, his cheeks damp with either tears or sweat or some guilt-steeped liquor of both, and fixated only on connecting the red dots, didn't notice the evening shadows lengthening—not until he reached for his flashlight and discovered he hadn't brought it.

There'd be no finding him in the dark. Tomorrow, Adi told himself. He'd return at first light. If the billy survived the night he'd dispense mercy in the morning; either way he'd find it.

Except, he realized, that he had no idea where he was at the moment. He'd only been paying attention to the blood trail itself, not the direction it was headed or the landscape it was dotting. From the gorge bottom he looked up at the purpling sky, where a few far-flung stars were beginning to emerge, and heard, one last time, the billy goat's cry as a long plaintive echo from the south. Adi's shoulders sank. This, right here, was surely where he belonged: alone in the earth's dungeon, clapped in irons for all his failures.

Only when he entered his hut, six hours later, after hiking through the dark to the island's southern tip and blindly clawing his way through a quagmire of mangroves, did he remember half the reason he'd gone afield that morning: to get food for E3. He went to the bird's box, with an apology on his tongue, but there was no sound from it: not the squeak with which E3 often greeted him nor the cardboard scuffing of its tiny feet.

He found his flashlight and shining it into the box let out a low wail. Inside were just feathers, strewn in front of the plastic Ninja Turtle, which had capsized onto its side, face to the cardboard wall. The rat, Adi knew at once. Oliver. Adi had left the T-shirt off the top of the box, and in his distracted preparations that morning had forgotten to replace it—and owing to that lapse, the Santa Flora Reed Warbler was truly extinct now. Because he'd believed Grejo wrong: that nature did give a fuck. But it was Adi who'd been wrong. Grejo had known it: and that, more than anything else, had been the meaning of his wave.

Adi curled himself on the floor beside the empty box but never slept. At some point during the night he thought he heard a rustling from the opening where he'd been feeding Oliver, but when he shone his flashlight on it there was nothing to see. He didn't know what if anything he'd have done had Oliver been perched there; a rat couldn't be anything but a rat, after all, as perhaps a man couldn't be anything but a man. Maybe existence yielded to its own semblance of gravity. The flashlight beam skated across the portrait of the old woman in the pince-nez glasses and lace bonnet. *Killers kill,* he heard her whispering.

Long before sunrise he wandered down to the cove with his horn to await first light. The seven nanny goats glanced up drowsily as he passed, Harmony blinking into his flashlight glare with what looked to Adi like almost maternal worry—for him or for her herd or for the billy goat he'd wounded, it wasn't clear and never could be. She declined to sing when he blew the horn, and without her voice the crude melodies felt brittle and vacant, less music than moan. So he set the horn beside him and sat in silence at the tide line, with his knees to his chest, until whitecaps started materializing out in the Pacific and the ash-colored clouds began revealing their tattered shapes. A rare wind was sloughing the island, causing an uneasy murmur to rise from the palms and the mangroves and the close-bitten bushes. Adi drank some cold instant coffee, ate from a can of salmon, suited up, reloaded the rifle, and was gone.

In the predawn murk the uncertain paths were even more uncertain; he let the gradients of the terrain guide him, up then down, down then up. From the outset he knew that finding the blood trail where he'd abandoned it would be impossible. When he'd given up the trail he'd been lost in the dark, with only dumb persistence having delivered him back to his hut. The only thing to do now was to return to where he'd shot the billy goat and retrace his steps. Yet even that might not be possible, he feared. A pewter mist was scudding across the island, and when at last dawn broke the sun hung smothered by a frayed shroud of low-hanging stratus. Even the merest drizzle would wash clean the blood trail. He quickened his pace.

He would finish off the billy goat, to end its suffering, and then quit. The satellite phone was inside his hut, its battery still fully charged. With a single call he could be off the island by nightfall. He'd say he was sick, or fake a twisted ankle. Or maybe he'd tell the truth: that the goats weren't to blame for what'd become of Santa Flora. That all they'd ever done was refuse to stop living. They'd eaten because they were hungry. They'd mated because life is something you pass down. They'd sung because it pleased them, to mark the island with their voices before etching it with their bones. They weren't a plague or a malignant growth or any of his interviewer's other fuming metaphors; they weren't metaphors at all. They were goats, nothing more, and their only crime had been to keep growing where we'd planted them. Santa Flora's degradation was as much mankind's doing as if we'd crop dusted it with gales of poison or leveled it with bombs or stacked its shores with condominiums. We'd ditched the goats here for our convenience, just as we'd dumped the trash washed up along the windward shore, then ignored them for a century and a half. You could slaughter every last goat but you couldn't eradicate the truth.

The clouds flexed and seethed, straining to muster rain, as Adi went scrambling forward, the island's pleats and promontories dingy in the vaporous half-light. In time he noticed the unusual absence of birds overhead. His rational mind told him they all must be hunkered down in advance of a storm, but Adi wasn't listening to reason; in his fevered imagination every bird on Santa Flora had been linked to every other bird via invisible nerve threads, all the swifts and the plovers and the pipers and the gulls and the warblers comprising a single mammoth organism, a million-winged nexus of life, and E3's death, its extinction, had wiped the skies clean of them. Adi's bumbling had killed them all.

The billy goat was likely dead too, he told himself. Except maybe Adi was telling himself that because he didn't want to face him, feared seeing his own conscience reflected in those wet, side-slanted eyes. What was worst for him, Adi asked himself: fear or pain or death itself? His one minuscule consolation, with Jairo, is that he'd never felt anything. Less than two seconds of confusion—Adi had done the math because he'd needed to know: the height, the mass, the velocity, the joules—then blackness.

The dampness thickened, almost clotted, as he reached the third and highest of the four ridges, the cloud deck so low that he could nearly reach it with a hand. He saw it condensing on the paddles of the cacti growing at this elevation, saw droplets slaloming between the thorns: a bleak omen for finding the blood trail and the wounded billy. Though it wasn't unfeasible, it occurred to him, for the billy goat to survive. He could be licking the bullet wound even now, nestled deep in the gorge and lap by steady lap marshaling back his old power and authority. Surely there was a chance. Adi recalled his grandfather marveling over the case of an old friend from his revolution days whose surgeon, during some routine procedure, had found and removed bullet fragments from where fifty years earlier he'd been shot at a protest. The friend kept the pieces inside a small jar that he liked showing off to waiters and barmen and other strangers.

Adi ascended the fourth and final ridge to where just ahead of him the island dropped into that amphitheater of cliffs. This was the place where he thought he'd shot the billy. Yes, this was it: he remembered the silver-olive bush the billy dived into and behind it the round bald rock where Adi had found the first blood spot. But the rock was glossed with condensed morning fog, rinsed clean of his failure. The island had commenced healing even if the billy goat hadn't.

Adi searched ahead. But even the pool in the alcove had faded into a weak brown stain, as if someone had emptied leftover coffee there. He stood staring at it. He'd failed, then failed again. He'd tried to save the world and then an island and then an extinct bird and then finally he'd tried saving a billy goat from pain that he himself had caused. He'd tried to save his son then afterward save his marriage. He'd tried saving himself. And in every last attempt, he'd done nothing but fail.

A sharp fast *bang* jolted him: a gunshot—for sure. It couldn't have been anything else. Instantly Adi fell to a crouch inside the alcove, swirling his head for any sign of where it'd come from. Had the shark finners changed course, and were shooting at him now? No other explanation fit. If so then he must've misinterpreted Grejo's wave: had it actually been a threat, a signal that they'd been hunting him ever since he'd fled and now had found him, the grin merely a manifestation of Grejo's appetite for killing, some lurid variation on licking his lips? Yes of *course,* Adi thought, notching another failure. They'd probably rounded the island's southern cape this morning, and finding his hut empty had tracked him up and down the island's rib cage far more swiftly and skillfully than he'd been tracking the wounded billy. They were going to kill him: for what he'd seen or who he was or for the capital do-goodism he represented or possibly for the mere brute sport of it, for the trophy of his candy shoes. They were going to kill him and sink him into the cove beside the shark and then tell jokes and light cigarettes. He backed himself deeper into the alcove and sat on his heels with the rifle atop his knees. He clicked off the safety and sat still and listened.

Another shot, *bang*. But absent the surprise of the first shot Adi was able to hear this one more clearly. It'd come from behind him, from down where the cliffs plunged, the shot too distant and oblique to be aimed his way. Whatever they were shooting at, it wasn't Adi. But then—what?

Creeping from the alcove he slid upward past the wet bloodless rock and through the silver-olive brush then up past where he'd shot the billy to where he'd watched them finning the shark, atop the southern rim of the cliff bowl. He didn't pause to fumble out his binoculars. This time he used the rifle scope to see.

The boat was anchored in the same spot as yesterday, and, like yesterday, the men were positioned at its stern. But the men weren't fishing. Chuky had a pistol in his hand, and whether from drunkenness or from the gathering waves jouncing the boat, both men were swaying and staggering. Adi watched him pass the pistol to Grejo, who made a theatrical show of aiming it at the island, like a duelist in an old-time movie, spreading his feet into a wide stance to stick himself to the deck. But a wave bounced the boat and sent him reeling into Chuky, who caught him and laughed and helped set him back upright. Yes, Adi decided: they were drunk. The sky behind them was boiling gray from the approaching storm but they seemed oblivious or indifferent to it. Adi could hear music coming from the boat, the faint booms of an electronic bass line. Grejo reprised his duelist's stance and fired.

Adi swung the scope leftward to track the shot then whispered, *No.* Spread two or three meters apart on a narrow ledge near the top of the cliff side were four goats. The men were taking drunken potshots at them, at four evenly spaced bull's-eyes pinned to the island. The lead goat, farthest out on the ledge, was bleating nonstop; Adi could hear her cries rising up the cliff sides, amplified by their concave shape. *No,* he whispered again.

He trained the crosshairs back onto the boat, where Grejo was shrugging off his miss and passing the pistol back to Chuky. With the scope, unlike the binoculars, Adi could see every detail, the five starfish legs tattooed upon Grejo's hand included. *German optics,* Chuky had said. *Bet you could see straight up a lizard's skirt with that scope.* Now it was Chuky's turn to shoot, and assuming the same duelist's pose with a cigarette drooping from his bottom lip he aimed the gun cliffward. *No,* Adi said, not whispering this time. The pistol cracked.

Where the bullet hit, Adi didn't see; but Chuky missed. The lead goat tried reversing but the ledge was thin and the goat behind her appeared confused and panicky, swinging her head back and forth while frantically bleating. She moved two steps forward, one step back, one step forward. *No,* Adi shouted, as her back hoof knocked loose rubble that went pouring down the cliff side. She hiked her leg back up, slipped again, recovered—

Adi clamped shut his eyes. He couldn't watch her fall. Couldn't bear hearing all the people on the sidewalk screaming and wailing and murmuring and tongue clicking, couldn't bear seeing them clumping together and pointing upward—not again. Couldn't bear lifting her soft broken body into his arms, feeling the limbs jellied and disjointed, couldn't bear seeing Deyanira's face when she trailed him out, the way it melted in shock, the way she'd clawed at Adi for possession of Jairo's limp body, the way his reedy arms flopped backward when she'd pulled him to her chest.

There'd been two boys from the apartment up there when Jairo sneaked to the roof. Yorly, sixteen, and Ronny, fourteen. Yorly with his homemade tattoos and Ronny with the ornate blue switchblade always glinting on his belt. Deyanira had for years fretted about raising Jairo around kids like them—complained about them loitering in front of the building, relayed rumors about packages swiped from the mail, said she'd heard them muttering *retard* in the elevator with her and Jairo—but the apartment was spacious and overlooked both the park and the city's tiny hub of jazz clubs and in the capital's real estate market a private schoolteacher's salary went only so far. The rooftop, everyone knew, was where Yorly and Ronny stole away to smoke weed and do whatever boys like them did on rooftops, which was only the slightest reason Jairo had always been forbidden to go up there.

All they ever knew was that Jairo ventured up to test a new paper plane he'd designed. Yorly and Ronny told the police he'd jumped. They said they didn't know why. They said retards did weird things.

Deyanira would never stop believing they'd pushed or thrown him over the side. But they hadn't: an old woman across the street saw Jairo fall and, looking up six stories, saw the boys' faces appear over the ledge a few moments later, their mouths carved into identically shocked Os. But then, Adi didn't believe Jairo had jumped or fallen of his own volition either. Yorly and Ronny had talked him into it, he felt sure: had assured Jairo he could fly just the same as his paper airplanes. *You're special,* he could hear them saying. *That's what your mama and papa say, isn't it? That you're special.* Giggling, stoned, daring him to prove he wasn't as stupid as they deemed him.

But Jairo hadn't been stupid. Except about the world, which he'd trusted too wholeheartedly, congenitally unable to conceive that anyone or anything could want to do him harm. His mind had never made room for complexity, for a dilemma's horns, for the way two wrongs could sometimes equal a right.

Grejo had the pistol now and in his other hand was brandishing a half-empty liter of aguardiente. The storm was edging closer, the mist turning to drizzle and forcing Adi to wipe the scope lenses dry. He shifted his sights to the cliff side, where the second goat had managed to scuttle backward but was blocked by the third, the two of them now fused into a larger, more inviting target, a double bull's-eye. Grejo assumed his stance.

No! Adi shouted, twice, but they couldn't hear him over the thump of the music and the crash of the waves lashing the boulders at the cliff base. He loosed his left hand from the rifle barrel and with just his right hand pointed the rifle skyward, the trigger mere centimeters from his head, and let out a shot. Immediately came a burst of pain on the right side of his skull, as if a firecracker had just detonated inside his ear. He slapped his left hand over it and hissed; the shot had ruptured his eardrum.

Blenching from the pain, he aimed the rifle back at the boat to peer through the wet scope. Both men were facing Adi now, screwing their gazes at where he was standing at the cliff edge. On their faces, perplexity morphed into glee. Grejo hoisted the bottle above his head and with a wide gap-toothed grin pointed it toward the goats on the cliff. Then he waved a hand from them to Adi and back again, very clearly inviting Adi to take a shot, to join their game, daring him to fly.

The gun Deyanira brought home two days later had come from her grandfather, the crime boss, one of the tools of a trade that Adi had always avoided learning about, willful ignorance having struck him as the least immoral course, given the circumstances. *Take it*, she'd said to him, holding it flat on her quivering palm the way you'd offer pills or coins. Night and day she'd been delirious with grief, unable to eat or sleep and sometimes collapsing to the floor as though fainting without losing consciousness, as though felled by electric jolts of grief. She'd looked down at the gun and up at Adi. *They murdered our son,* she'd said.

Over and over again he'd refused, lifting his hands above his head and stepping backward as though even to touch the gun would be to accede. He wasn't a killer, he told her, didn't live by that code. He couldn't slaughter someone else's children no matter what they'd done to his child. And what exactly they'd done wasn't fully clear and never would be, however bone-deep Adi's suspicions lay. And what he couldn't add, to her, was that some fraction of the blame was Jairo's: for trusting what the boys were telling him, for failing to fathom any reason they'd be lying, for joining his father for eleven years in pretending the world cared for him, cushioned him, gave a fuck. *That won't undo it,* he'd tried telling her, *Dey, nothing can undo it,* his refusal causing her entire body to shake so violently, approaching a seizure, that he feared she'd turn the gun on him or herself or both. A day later, instead, she left, packing her clothes and Jairo's into four rolling suitcases that her brothers carried silently down to the sidewalk for her without ever making eye contact with Adi. Several weeks later a neighbor told him that Yorly and Ronny had been grabbed on the street one night, by two older men they didn't recognize, and beaten to the pavement with baseball bats. Her grandfather's men, Adi guessed.

Both men were waving to Adi from the stern now, urging him to take a shot. They cheered as he swung the barrel toward the cliff side, where the lead goat was still bleating. He saw the men slumping in disappointment, however, when he swung the barrel back their way.

Adi raised his gaze from the scope to scan the cliff side with his naked eye, ignoring the pain piercing his ear as he searched for some route he could take to get to the goats, to cast himself beside them on the ledge and shield them. But no such route was visible, not for a human, and since the goats would doubtlessly misunderstand his intentions he'd only be endangering them further. And as drunk as the men appeared to be, they might just shoot him anyway.

He saw a small blast of rock explode as Grejo took his shot, saw chips and splinters of it showering the two goats beneath. It'd hit just a meter above their heads; despite their drunkenness, and despite the bobbing seas, the men were dialing in their shots. It was only a matter of time.

Adi wiped the scope's lenses dry and returned its crosshairs to the boat. Grejo was laughing, almost doubled over, pinching together his fingers to show

how close his shot had been, first to Chuky and then up at Adi. He passed the pistol to Chuky and then brought the bottle to his lips for a deep slug. Owing to the toss of the boat Adi's crosshairs glided over nearly every sea creature in the inked aquarium of Grejo's body, the jellyfish on his cheek, the manta ray spread across his breastbone, the tiger shark pulsing on his neck with every swallow. Chuky extended his arm to aim and squeezed shut one eye.

Not until that moment, with his eardrum stabbing and the drizzle finally strengthening into rain, did Adi understand, with a thunderclap of clarity, what saving Santa Flora meant. *The job is removing a malignant growth that's been steadily erasing some of the most vulnerable and least studied flora and fauna on the bloody planet,* he heard her saying. *That's the job. That's what it is.* He dropped down to a kneel behind the very same low slab of obsidian he'd been hiding behind the day before and steadied the barrel atop its smooth crown, pinning the crosshairs to Chuky's chest. Then he blew the air from his lungs and fired.

Chuky lurched backward, the pistol flying from his hand as he went windmilling into the cabin and then slid down against it. Inside the scope Adi watched Grejo staring down at Chuky kicking his legs beside the heap of fins, and then look up at him, up at Adi, in flat bewilderment, as though struggling to make any sense of a world that only, in that moment, made sense to Adi. The rain began gusting. Adi jerked up the titanium bolt handle, pulled back the bolt then pushed it back in, emptied his lungs, and without a single question in his mind shot again.

ABOUT THE AUTHOR

JONATHAN MILES is the author of the novels *Dear American Airlines* and *Want Not*, both *New York Times* Notable Books, and the novel *Anatomy of a Miracle: The True* Story of a Paralyzed Veteran, a Mississippi Convenience Store, a Vatican Investigation, and the Spectacular Perils of Grace*. His journalism, essays, and criticism have appeared in a wide variety of publications, including *The New York Times*, where he served as a columnist. In 2024, he toured as a multi-instrumentalist in the band of the Grammy-winning artist Jon Batiste. He currently serves as writer in residence at the Solebury School in New Hope, Pennsylvania.